AF241253

MURDER IN THE TOWER: JACK'S JOURNAL #2

ALSO BY NELLIE H. STEELE

Cate Kensie Mysteries:

The Secret of Dunhaven Castle

Murder at Dunhaven Castle

Holiday Heist at Dunhaven Castle

Jack's Journal:

The Secret Keepers

Shadow Slayers Stories:

Shadows of the Past

Stolen Portrait Stolen Soul

Gone

Maggie Edwards Adventures

Cleopatra's Tomb

Secret of the Ankhs

Duchess of Blackmoore Mysteries

Death of a Duchess

MURDER IN THE TOWER: JACK'S JOURNAL #2

A CATE KENSIE MYSTERY

NELLIE H. STEELE

A Novel Idea Publishing

This is a work of fiction. Names, characters, places, and incidents either are the product of the author's imagination or are used fictitiously. Any resemblance to actual persons, living or dead, events, or locales is entirely coincidental.

Copyright © 2021 by Nellie H. Steele

All rights reserved.

No part of this book may be reproduced in any form or by any electronic or mechanical means, including information storage and retrieval systems, without written permission from the author, except for the use of brief quotations in a book review.

All rights reserved.

Cover design by Stephanie A. Sovak.

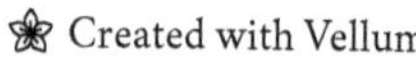 Created with Vellum

ACKNOWLEDGMENTS

A very special thank you to everyone who made this book possible! Special shout outs to: Stephanie Sovak, Paul Sovak, Michelle Cheplic, Mark D'Angelo, Lori D'Angelo and Peter Nicholls.

Finally, a HUGE thank you to you, the reader!

Reid Family Tree

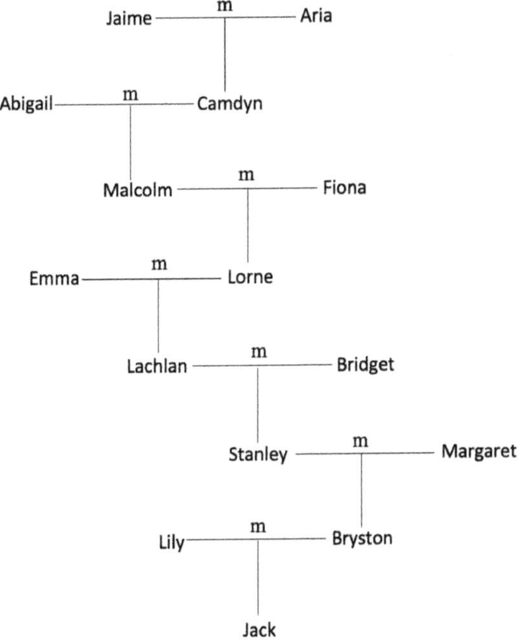

CHAPTER 1

September 26

7:15 p.m.

*H*ere's where it really starts. It's been a little over a month since I last wrote in this journal. I almost assumed I was safe! After Cate and I learned the incredible truth about the castle and its hidden secret, we took some time to settle in. Cate began research on her new asset and her ancestors. The local librarian and town gossip, Mrs. Campbell, also twisted Cate's arm to host a giant Halloween party on the grounds.

With all the work for this major event, I assumed Cate's mind and most of our waking hours would be devoted to the party. After all, it required the use of the ballroom. The last time anyone used the ballroom was likely two Countesses ago! We'd also want the grounds to look sharp. It'd be the first time we welcomed guests onto Dunhaven's grounds in decades!

Earlier today, I worked on a few items that needed tending near the ballroom when Lady Cate sought me out.

"Lady Cate!" I said as she rounded the corner and approached me. "And how are you today?" I assumed she had another list of to-be-completed items from everyone's favorite party planner, Isla Campbell.

"I'm good, how are you?" Cate inquired. That's when I noticed the sparkle in her eye. This wasn't about the upcoming party. Cate had something else on her mind.

"Well, I was fine, but you've got that mischievous look in your eye so I'm betting I won't be in a few minutes."

Cate frowned at me. "I have no such look," she claimed.

Perhaps the lassie didn't realize it, but she DEFINITELY had a look.

"No? Then what's that in your hand?" I asked referencing the folder she held. "Just some random paperwork that you happen to be carrying about?"

"Just a few articles about a former castle owner. I wanted to get your impression on it."

"My impression, huh?" I doubted that. Cate had a plan. And one I probably wouldn't like. I grabbed the folder from her and gave a quick scan of the articles inside. The first one, entitled MURDER AT DUNHAVEN CASTLE, detailed a suspected murder on the estate during a Halloween ball in 1856. A footman was found dead. Details were few and far between given the recentness of the murder. The body of one Andrew Forsythe had been found near the turret after having fallen from the window three stories up. The fall, though, did not kill the young man. Instead, his skull had been bashed in.

I scanned the next article. It detailed a stunning turn of events. When the police arrived to search the castle for evidence, the castle's proprietor, Randolph MacKenzie, confessed to the crime. He cited a fit of jealous, drunken rage over the perception that the footman and his wife shared an intimate glance. Lord MacKenzie, who had previously provided an alibi for the time of the murder, stunned police with his confession. He maintained his conscience did not allow him to continue his ruse. The remaining articles in the folder detailed his trial and the subsequent fallout. Despite his alibi being corroborated by several witnesses, Lord MacKenzie was convicted and sentenced to death. He left behind his wife and infant son.

I flicked the folder closed. "Well?" Cate questioned.

"My impression is this Randolph fellow got in a jealous rage and killed someone, then he couldn't live with the guilt, confessed and they sentenced him to death."

Cate frowned at me. She didn't approve of my explanation. To be honest, I'm not sure I did either, but I approved of it more than time traveling to discover another explanation. "Really? It doesn't strike you as odd?"

"No?" I answered. It seemed plausible. "Perhaps he was a hothead, or maybe his wife was having an affair. I don't find it that strange."

"It doesn't make sense," Cate said. She paced the floor in front of me as she detailed her case. She'd given this quite a bit of thought. She wasn't going to let this one go. "It's all too convenient. He has an alibi then out of the blue he confesses? He leaves his beloved wife to raise his infant son alone while he rots in prison awaiting the death penalty. Why would he do that? He would have gotten away with murder by just letting his alibi stand."

She had a point, though there were any number of reasons why someone may do an about-face in this situation. "Possibly someone threatened to tell, or he didn't expect someone in his position would get that kind of sentence. Could be any number of things, who knows?"

"Well, Randolph knows, and perhaps a few others," Cate answered with that twinkle in her eye that made my blood run cold.

"Cate…" I began.

Cate interrupted me. "I'm just saying maybe something else was going on there and we should check into it."

"Caaaaaaaaate," I chided.

"And we have the capability to check into it. The year in the article is one of the access points your grandfather told us about."

"CATE!" I exclaimed. "Are you kidding me?"

"Come on, Jack! My ancestor was accused of murder and was put to death! What if he was innocent?"

"First, he confessed, he wasn't accused," I corrected. "And second, what if he wasn't? You're willing to risk our lives to find out if he's innocent?"

Cate made a face at me. "How are we risking our lives, Jack? All I'm suggesting is that we go back and take a peek around, perhaps prevent a murder, perhaps save an innocent man's life."

Oh, only that, huh, I pondered. This was trouble waiting to happen. Anything could occur. We could permanently alter history! We could erase ourselves from the timeline. We could die in 1856 before we were even born!

"Do you remember, Cate, the conversation we shared with my grandfather about not changing history when we first learned about this? Because I do. What if we change history so much that one or both of us disappear? We shouldn't be messing around with this stuff."

"I won't do anything that will jeopardize our lives," Cate promised.

"That's the point, Cate. You don't know what tiny thing you might do that would jeopardize our lives! There's a butterfly effect."

"Where is your sense of adventure?" Cate prodded, trying a new tactic.

"My sense of adventure?" I questioned. "My sense of

adventure is ordering something other than the fish and chips at the pub. Not romping around in other time periods solving murders!"

"So, you agree the murder needs to be solved!" Cate exclaimed.

Oh, I'd stuck my foot in it this time. "Bah, Cate! I won't win this argument, will I?"

"Probably not," Cate admitted. "Let's just look around, at least. We have a month before the murder. We'll see who the players are and if anything seems amiss."

"Only that, huh?" I answered. I didn't buy it, but I wasn't going to win this one. Perhaps it would be interesting.

"Hey, I'd go myself, but it's against the rules."

"Wonderful, now you're concerned with the rules. I guess that's something at least, you're obeying one rule. Okay, okay. So, when do you want to go?"

"Hmm," Cate pondered. "Well, it's September twenty-sixth. We'll have a little over one month before the murder. How about Sunday? Perhaps we can take a quick peek around while most everyone in the household is at church? Get the lay of the land before we move on to trying to figure out what happened."

"Sunday it is, I guess," I agreed. I considered this a terrible idea, but a small part of me got a tiny bit excited. To be clear, a minuscule part.

"Excellent! Glad you agree!"

"Oh, I far from agree," I informed Cate. "I'm a conscientious objector, but I'll do it. If only to be sure I stop you from erasing some vital part of history by accident."

She rolled her eyes at me. "You're so dramatic," she said with a laugh.

"Says the person who suspects a centuries-old murder, that has been solved, I might add, has some dark secret lurking in it that still needs solving."

"We shall see," Cate said. "I'll get everything ready for Sunday! I'll let you get back to work!"

It was my turn to roll my eyes. "Fantastic, on both counts."

As Cate wandered away, I stared after her. What had I gotten myself into? Another trip through time. This time not just for a quick peek around. Sure, our first trip wouldn't be too terrible. At least, that was my sincere hope. But it wouldn't end there! Solving a murder?! I wasn't sure I was up for this.

With a sigh, I returned to my work. I had all the way until Sunday to push it to the depths of my mind.

As I settled in front of my TV for the night, my mind preferred not to cooperate with me. Try as I might, the pending investigation shoved itself to the front of my mind.

The TV show droned on in the background as I considered the details. Randolph MacKenzie, lord of the manor, killed a man, or so it appeared. He confessed to the crime. But first, he'd given an alibi. A solid one, it seemed. Several others had corroborated his statements. Perhaps they were loyal servants, perhaps they had been threatened.

Had Randolph's alibi been a farce? Suppose it was. That would mean he killed a man over a shared glance with his wife. Crimes of passion were not uncommon. It could be true. But was it? Had Victoria MacKenzie engaged in an extramarital affair and stoked the wrath of her husband enough to lead to murder?

Perhaps this was an excuse. Perhaps Randolph had some sordid business dealings with the man that had gone wrong. I decided it was entirely possible for Randolph MacKenzie to have murdered someone for any number of reasons. We had no idea what kind of temperament he had. Perhaps he was a hothead. He certainly had a reputation to this day with the town gossips who maintained that he engaged in all sorts of shameful behavior. The story that he kept a woman locked in the tower room made its way around the town over a century after he lived.

Still, Cate had a point. He gave the police an alibi. That alibi was confirmed by several others. He could have gotten away with murder had he merely left it stand. He confessed because his conscience wouldn't allow him to remain silent. Would a man prone to these types of base behaviors confess to a crime when he was poised to get away with murder?

No, I decided. As much as I hated to admit it, Cate was correct. Randolph MacKenzie could be innocent. And now it was our job to prove it.

CHAPTER 2

September 28
9:03 p.m.

Tomorrow we time travel. Earlier this evening, we met to discuss some of the details for the trip. I took Pap along with me, hoping he'd talk Cate out of this hare-brained scheme. He didn't. I'll record our discussion in case I need to refer to the details later. Then I'm going to try to get some sleep. I doubt I will. The prospect of time travel is not as thrilling to me as it is to Cate. She seems downright giddy!

The best part of the night was playing with Riley! Mrs. Fraser had given him a bone and we played a game of tug of war with it until the little rascal stole it away from me. "She's all yours, Riley," I told him. "You're one tough little mutt!"

"Perhaps in his mind, you owe him one since he lost his last one running around the yard searching for you," Cate said.

"Oh?" I asked.

"Yes," Cate answered, "Mrs. Fraser gave him one Thursday. When we returned to the kitchen to check on him, he was gone. We found him outside minus his bone. He must have run out of the door looking for you and lost his bone during his search. Did he ever find you?"

"Thursday? No, I was inside that day. I never saw him."

"Hmm, that's right. Funny he didn't realize you were in here. Oh well, at least he's got his replacement, he's happy," Cate said as we watched Riley settle on the floor, chewing his bone. "It's nice to see you again, Mr. Reid," Cate said, turning her attention to Pap.

"Aye, it's always a pleasure to see you too, lassie!"

"Has Jack brought you up to speed on my request?"

"Aye. I told him all about your insane plan," I answered first.

"It's not insane!" Cate objected. Turning back to Pap, she said, "We were hoping you might have some information for us about that time period. Did you and either Mary or Gertrude travel back to that time?"

"Now, wait a minute, lassie, I want to discuss some estate business with you before you dive into this discussion and lose all sense of reality," I said.

Cate frowned at me but allowed me to finish my business. I at least wanted to do SOME estate business. We'd told everyone we were meeting to handle it and I didn't want to be a liar!

"Okay, that's done," Cate said, "now let's move on to the fun stuff."

"That was the fun stuff," I said with a grin.

"Only you consider bills and business 'fun stuff' and not time travel."

"Only you consider going back to a time when people died of typhoid in their mid-thirties and indoor plumbing was nonexistent 'fun stuff,'" I retorted.

"Hey, consider this though, if you were estate manager back then you'd have one less thing to worry about!"

"You two make quite the pair, don't you?" Pap said with a laugh. Apparently, he found our bickering humorous!

"Speaking of estate managers, I guess besides your ancestors, we may run into some of ours, huh?" I wasn't sure how I felt about meeting my ancestors. Perhaps this was the silver lining in time travel.

"Yes," Cate said, opening her research folder. "I charted your family tree. Your great-great-great-grandfather, Malcolm Reid, was the estate manager under Randolph MacKenzie. It would be him we'd have the chance to meet. Malcolm and Randolph grew up together before Malcolm became Randolph's estate manager." She pulled out a small drawing of a family tree and handed it to me.

"Wow, look at you with our family tree!" I said as I perused the paper. "Take a look, Pap! She's got us all mapped out." I handed the paper over to Pap.

"Aye, she has," he answered. "And it looks about right to me. Well done, Lady Cate, well done!"

Cate beamed. "It took a little work, but I was able to track everything down through household documents and some information that you gave me, Mr. Reid. You are a wealth of knowledge!"

"Yeah, he is," I agreed. "If I'm lucky he'll even have enough to stave off your crazy plan."

"Crazy plan?" Pap questioned.

"Yeah, Pap, Cate's got another one of her brilliant ideas to time travel."

"Ah, time traveling, what a rush that was," Pap answered. He sounded as though he almost missed it. My brow furrowed at his reaction.

"Bah, don't feed into her Pap, you'll only make her worse," I chided.

Cate laughed. "So, tell me this crazy plan you've got, Lady Cate!" Pap requested.

"Isla Campbell gave me a few articles from the year 1856, one of the time periods we can travel to, which makes them intriguing to begin with. But what makes them even more intriguing is the tale of murder I read."

"Oh, aye, you mean the murder of that servant by Lord MacKenzie," he said, nodding his head as he remembered.

"Right. That's the story I mean, but I'm not convinced Lord MacKenzie murdered that man. Hence my desire to time travel. I want to investigate."

"Ah, you think he's innocent?" Pap inquired.

"That she does, Pap, and she's dead set on proving it, too."

"What makes you think that, lassie?"

"A hunch. It doesn't add up. He first says he's innocent, he has a solid alibi, then out of the blue and in a complete reversal, he confesses to the murder and is sentenced to death, leaving behind his infant son and beloved wife. It just doesn't make sense."

My grandfather considered the information.

"Well?" Jack prodded.

"Well, she's got a point."

"Hey, whose side are you on?" I joked.

"I've been the voice of reason long enough, laddie, I'm retired! Now I can voice my opinion. And the lassie has a point."

"Isn't it more probable that old Randolph's guilt got to him and he confessed rather than live with it?" I questioned.

"What about his alibi?" Cate tossed back.

"Someone lied to protect him?" I answered, forming my response as a question.

"More than one someone, several people saw him."

"It's not inconceivable," I said.

Cate rolled her eyes at me. "We have a way to find out."

I glanced to Pap for help but he shrugged his shoulders at me. "It's your show now, Jackie. Yours and Cate's."

I sighed, rolling my eyes. "Some help you are."

"Do you know anything else about this story, Mr. Reid?" Cate queried.

Pap glanced into the air above him as if searching for an answer. "Not much more than you summarized earlier. Lady Mary and I traveled to that time. They had many a great party on the estate before Randolph's trouble. Lady Victoria was quite the entertainer! I don't know any facts about this though, we didn't speak with Randolph about it, nor did we do any investigating of our own."

Cate raised her eyebrows at me. "Well, it looks like it's up to us to do some investigating!"

I shrugged at her. "Guess I'm not talking you out of it, huh?"

"Nope," Cate answered.

"And I guess you're not going to talk any sense into her?" I said, directing the question to Pap.

"To quote the lady, 'nope,'" he said with a chuckle.

"Ahhhh, well okay then, let's get on with the history lesson so I know the players," I acquiesced. "Malcolm was the estate manager for Randolph MacKenzie, you said?"

"Right, and Randolph was the son of Finlay and Moira MacKenzie, grandson of Douglas, who built the castle and discovered the time travel anomaly. The concept was probably still novel to them."

"Anything that we should know about Randolph except that he's a crazy murderer?"

"Hey!" Cate said, batting her hand at me, "that's my ancestor you're slandering there! And, yes, Randolph had quite the reputation before the murder."

"How so?" I asked, taking a sip of my ale.

"Womanizer," Pap chimed in.

"Yes, according to Mrs. Campbell, Randolph garnered quite the reputation. He spent a good bit of time overseas and the rumor was that he brought home a young woman with him. The story is he kept her in the tower room to satisfy his 'more base desires' in the words of Mrs. Campbell," Cate said.

"Any record of the girl existing?" I asked.

"None that I've found so far."

"So possibly just some tall tales from the village," I suggested.

"It could be, but there's usually some truth in a rumor, some reason that started it."

"Most likely an old big-mouthed biddy like Mrs. Campbell," I quipped.

Cate scowled at me. "She isn't that bad!"

"If you say so. Okay, so who else are we trying to avoid?"

"Funny," Cate said, groaning. "Also in the household was Victoria, Randolph's wife."

"Anything of note about Victoria?"

"Victoria MacKenzie, neé Winston, was from a well-known and powerful English family. She was also a countess, so she made a lateral move marrying Randolph, although some would have said she stepped down because she moved out of English aristocracy settling for a Scottish lord rather than an English one."

History lesson, blech. I stared straight ahead, then let my head drop to my chest, feigning snoring.

"Okay, okay, I get it, here's the juicy bit," Cate said with a roll of her eyes. "Victoria had no shortage of suitors. Her family was not only wealthy and powerful, but she was renowned for her beauty throughout England."

"Aye, she was a real beauty, that one!" Pap added.

"So, what made the beautiful Victoria leave the English high society for Scotland?" I asked.

"She moved to Scotland and married Randolph because he spent countless months wooing her. He wrote her letters, poems, and sonnets. He visited daily when he was within her vicinity. Even if she refused to see him, he'd leave her a love note and come right back the next day."

"Looks like his persistence paid off."

"It did, she eventually succumbed to his considerable charm and married him. They had a son, Ethan, in the same year that the murder occurred. He was only nine months old."

"So, when did he bring this supposed girl back?" I questioned.

"The rumor mill said he brought her back from his honeymoon," Pap answered.

"What? Oh, come on, he was so in love with the beautiful Victoria that he brought back another woman from his honeymoon?" I complained.

"Yes, it seems rather quick that he tired of her when he was so persistent, right?" Cate said.

"Which makes me think that rumor is just that, a rumor."

"I guess we could find out tomorrow, take a swing by the old tower room and check," Cate joked.

"Caaaaaaaate," I admonished.

Cate held her hands up in defeat. "Okay, okay, we won't go into the tower room tomorrow."

I grimaced at her, noting that she only agreed not to go into the tower room TOMORROW. "Anyone else?"

"Yes, Randolph had a ne'er-do-well brother that hung around the house many times. His name was Lorne. He wasn't a permanent resident at the castle. He would check in at times with a random woman."

"Perhaps he brought the tower girl?"

"No, that rumor was definitely about Randolph. Lorne seemed like the type that wouldn't bother hiding a girl in the tower room. He had numerous affairs none of which he kept secret. Other than those three, a random girl that Lorne brought home, and the staff, there shouldn't have been anyone else at the castle in those days. Randolph and Lorne had a sister, but she died of influenza when she was only fifteen."

"How did you find this information?"

"Various sources, some from Randolph's letters to Victoria that she kept, some from letters they wrote when he was in prison. Others from my book research, local legends, family histories, et cetera."

"Good work, Cate. Now, I think we need a few ground rules and a backstory, in case we run into someone."

"Rules?" Cate said with a dismayed expression.

"Yes, rules. Rule one: we're only going to look around. YOUR words," I said as Cate opened her mouth to protest. "IF, and this is an enormous IF, we discover anything amiss, we return. Upon our return, we will discuss how to proceed, if at all. Agreed?"

"Okay, fine," Cate sighed. "I agree to just get the lay of the land, so that's what we'll do tomorrow."

"And if someone catches us, what's the backstory?"

"Backstory?"

"Yes, Cate, the backstory, who are we? Why we're there? You can't very well say 'Hello, I'm Cate Kensie, I'm a time-traveling history professor and this is my friend, Jack. Mind if we have a look-see?'"

Pap chuckled at the conversation.

"Wandered in by accident?" Cate kidded, shrugging her shoulders.

I made a face. "I don't think that will work."

"We could say we're some distant cousin. Families traveled all the time to stay with each other, often they arrived without notice because correspondence was delayed or lost."

"Okay, so I'm some kind of distant cousin to the MacKenzies?" I asked.

"Well, both of us."

"Both of us? That makes no sense."

"Why not? We could be siblings."

"Oh, right, that'll work. Hello, I'm Jack MacKenzie," I practiced, pretending to shake someone's hand, "your distant Scottish cousin, and this is my American sister, Cate."

"I could try a Scottish accent, mate," Cate said in her best imitation of a Scot.

My eyes went wide at the attempt and I glanced to my grandfather before we both burst into laughter. "Do you want to get us caught?" I said when I recovered.

"I thought that was passable."

"Lassie, you couldn't pass for Scottish with that accent if you dressed head to toe in tartan, carried bagpipes, and had your clan crest tattooed on your forehead," I said, still chuckling.

Also still laughing, Pap agreed, "Aye, lassie, that's terrible."

Cate rolled her eyes. "Okay, smartypants, how do we explain me then."

"Ah, my wife?" I readied for a slap on this one. Instead, Cate frowned. "Hey," I said as I sipped at my ale, "I saw that. I'm quite a catch, I'll have you know. Besides, it would make sense why you're American then and why we are together."

"Yes," Cate agreed, "it wouldn't be very proper if I was running around the Scottish countryside with a man."

"Nay, they'd think you're one of Lorne's girls," I said, letting out another big laugh.

"Okay, so there we are. We are the MacKenzies, distant cousins to Randolph in for a visit. Didn't you get our letter?" Cate practiced feigning shock.

"And the Emmy goes to…" I teased. "Well, I guess we have

everything then. Looks like we're ready to travel to 1856, or at least as ready as we'll ever be."

"I suppose I'll need to dig up a fake wedding ring, but other than that we're ready!" Cate said, raising her glass in a toast.

"Good luck to you two. Can I get a copy of this family tree? You've got it so neatly written," Pap asked, admiring the lineage.

"Sure! I'll make a copy for you now."

"All right, I will see you tomorrow then, bright and early," I said as she handed off the copy.

We made our way home after a slight delay. Little Riley had gone missing. We found him outside the kitchen door. Mr. Fraser suggested the little bugger might be sneaking off to bury his bones. With that mystery solved, I dropped Pap at his cottage and returned home for a sleepless night.

CHAPTER 3

September 29
1:18 p.m.

ow! We time traveled today. Details of our little journey are below. I realize I've known about this for over a month, but... This was the first time we've actually time-traveled while knowing what we were doing and doing it on purpose!

I was certain I wouldn't enjoy it at all, especially after I slipped into the garb we had to wear to fit in. I sincerely hoped we wouldn't get caught, but just in case, we had to be dressed in appropriate clothing for the 1850s. The attire lacked any comfort at all. As I slipped into my car, I was glad no one drove past to see me dressed like this. I couldn't wait until I was home and back in my sweats.

I gazed up at the castle as I approached it on the long drive. What would the place look like in the 1850s? We were about to find out. My stomach turned over as I considered the prospect. Nervousness filled me as I parked the car, and approached the door.

I stepped through into the foyer. Cate made her way down the stairs in a large bell-shaped dress.

"Thought I'd let myself in the front door since I'm a MacKenzie now," I joked.

"Funny," Cate answered. "The clothes worked well!"

"I'm not so sure about that, although, I think you look nice in your dress."

Cate curtsied dramatically. "Why thank you, kind sir!" she said with a laugh.

I tugged at my collar. "Boy, these are uncomfortable. I'm glad I live in this century."

"Mine aren't much better," Cate admitted. "Okay, ready to go?"

"No," I said, "but I don't think I've got a choice."

"You haven't, come on!" Cate said. She led the way up the main staircase. She plodded along at a slow pace.

"Wow, so there IS something that can slow down the great Catherine Kensie!" I joked.

"Yes, this dress is not comfortable, let me tell you. It weighs a ton! I'll have no trouble sleeping tonight after all the exercise from lugging this weight around."

We wound through the halls to the bedroom where Cate disappeared. In a creative move, we termed it the "1850s bedroom." Sweat formed across my forehead as we approached the closet. Cate grinned at me and with a deep breath, she held the timepiece in front of her. "Okay, let's do this!"

I held my hand as steady as I could as I wrapped it around Cate's and rubbed the timepiece. The second hand slowed to a crawl. As it crept around the face, Cate said, "Guess we're here."

"Guess so," I answered. I glanced around and swallowed hard.

"Okay, well, let's go explore!" Cate started for the closed

closet door.

"Wait a minute, Cate!" I said as I pulled her back.

"What?" she asked.

"At least let me check everything out before we plow out into the house!" I shoved her behind me and crept to the door. Reids were meant to protect their MacKenzie counterparts, and I was determined to do my duty.

I cracked the door open a slit and glanced into the bedroom. All clear. Another bead of perspiration formed on my brow as we crept into the room. I inched the bedroom door open and peered into the hall.

"Well?" Cate whispered behind me.

"Coast's clear for the moment," I breathed.

"Okay, let's go!" Cate said. She flanked me and darted into the hallway. I followed her with a roll of my eyes. My guard dog status would be well earned with Cate at the helm.

"What are we looking around for, Cate?" I asked as I followed her. She seemed to have a specific destination in mind.

"Anything that gives us some information about Randolph and company, like journals or handwritten notes. Anything that can shed some information on the stories that surrounded Randolph and the castle in Randolph's time."

"And where do you propose we search for this?"

"I thought we'd start in the office. All his correspondence is likely there. We can rifle through the desk."

We navigated the empty halls to the office. Cate headed straight for the paper-covered desk. Organization seemed to be a skill Randolph lacked. I took a post at the door, eyeing the hall in case anyone appeared. Cate scanned through the documents on the desk. She moved on to the drawers.

"Jack!" Cate whispered.

"Yeah?" I asked, glancing over my shoulder at her.

"Check in those files over there for anything that might

be of interest." She pointed toward a pile of papers stacked on top of an old-fashioned file cabinet. I preferred to stay on watch at the door, but I figured it would expedite the search if I pitched in.

Cate finished her search of the desk. She sidled next to me as I perused the final file in my stack. "Anything?" she questioned.

"Only employment records and investments and so on. Nothing that would shed any light on your mystery. How about you?"

"Nothing," she answered.

Good enough. Time to go! "Okay, let's head back," I suggested.

"Wait a minute!" she said. I groaned internally. "There are more places to check."

I tugged at my collar, suddenly feeling overheated. "Such as? I don't like gallivanting around here."

"We should still have time. The church service shouldn't be over. Let's check Victoria's bedroom."

I rolled my eyes again but followed Cate to the upstairs bedroom. After a quick search, we found Victoria's room. Cate located a journal. Though after the birth of Victoria and Randolph's son, it did little to shed any light on the current mystery. At least it didn't indicate any torrid affairs with the footman in question.

"Okay, Cate, fun's over, let's go," I insisted after she replaced the journal.

With a frown, Cate trudged back to the 1850s bedroom. As we navigated the halls, we passed the circular stairway leading to the tower room. Cate hesitated. Oh no, I thought. I stopped a few steps away and prodded for her to follow. "Cate, let's go!"

She didn't answer me. And she didn't move to follow me. Instead, she stared up that curving stone staircase as though it held all the answers. I recognized the gears spinning in that little head of hers, and I wasn't in agreement. "Cate, no! No way!" I insisted.

"But this is why we came!" she countered. I knew it! I knew she wanted to go to that room!

"No, Cate. It's too dangerous," I told her.

"How is it dangerous?" she queried.

"What if someone is in there? What do you propose we do, Cate? Open the door and say hello and introduce ourselves?"

"No, but we could listen at the door and determine if it sounds like someone is in there. If there're any signs it's inhabited."

"Let's go home," I pleaded.

"Oh, come on, one little listen and we can go, I promise," Cate said. She started up the stairs.

"Cate? Wait! Damn it!" I mumbled as I tore up the steps after her.

Cate reached the top before me and pressed her ear against the door. Puffing with exertion, I caught up to her a moment later. "Well? Do you hear any signs of life?" I asked.

Cate scowled. "No."

I raised my eyebrows at her. "Really? Aw shucks. Okay, let's go." Cate glowered at me. "Come on, you promised," I reminded her.

"Okay," she agreed with a sigh.

We started down the steps when I froze. I threw my arm out in front of Cate to bar her progress. "What is it?" she whispered.

My brow furrowed as my stomach turned over. I held my finger to my lips and mimed that I heard footsteps. Cate's eyes widened, confirming my auditory skills. Cate wore a mask of panic as the footfalls approached our location. We were trapped.

A closet laid between us and the source of the footsteps. We had to act fast before the person rounded the bend. Cate flashed a key from her dress pocket. I recognized the skeleton key for the castle. I snatched it from her hand and raced toward the door. Cate followed, pressing close to me as I unlocked and opened the door. I shoved Cate inside before entering and easing the door shut.

We pressed against the door and listened as we both held our breath. The footfalls passed us, continuing up the staircase toward the tower room. Cate signaled to me to open the door and identify the owner of the noise. I shook my head to declare an emphatic silent no. Cate nodded at me, signaling an equally vigorous yes. I rolled my eyes at her as I gave in and eased the door open a crack.

We both hovered at the door and peered out through the small gap. I spotted the figure of a man fiddling with a set of keys in one hand. He held a tray with a saucer and a teacup in the other. The man glanced down the stairs before inserting a key into the lock and entering the tower room.

As his face came into full view, Cate gasped, shrinking away from the door.

I furrowed my brow as I studied the man. Thick, dark, wavy hair covered his head and thick eyebrows shrouded his deep-set, dark eyes in an angular, chiseled face. "Who is that?" I whispered.

"That," Cate breathed back, "is Randolph MacKenzie."

The door closed behind Randolph. "We better make a run for it," I suggested.

There was little resistance on Cate's part. She pushed out the door before the words were out of my mouth and began her sprint down the stairs, carrying the awkward mounds of fabric as best she could. I followed and together we made a dash to the 1850s bedroom.

My heart was pounding as I grabbed Cate's hand and pulled her into the closet. "Let's go home," I insisted.

We used the timepiece to return to the present time. "Oh, thank God," I said the moment it reached normal speed.

"Close call," Cate admitted.

"Too close," I answered.

"But well worth it."

We definitely did not think in the same way. "How do you figure that?"

"We have the answer to one of our questions!" Cate said with a smile. I still didn't understand. "Randolph MacKenzie is most definitely keeping someone in the tower room."

I groaned. "A fine time for him to be visiting that person, too. He was supposed to be at church!"

"He must have stayed home to visit her. What better time to do so? The entire household, including his wife, is away."

"Well, are you satisfied?" I asked as my heart returned to normal speed and I loosened the uncomfortable, stiff collar from around my neck.

"Not in the slightest. The mystery deepens! We've established he's got someone in the tower. Why? Who?"

"Most likely a girl like the town gossips said," I answered. Cate didn't respond. She stalked away, her finger on her lips as she pondered in silence. I was beginning to hate when she was silent. "Caaaaaate," I warned.

"I need to do more research before…" she began.

I interrupted her. "Before you give up?" I asked with hope in my voice.

"No, before we go back."

I groaned. "I was afraid you'd say that."

"Look on the bright side, Jack," Cate replied.

"What's that?"

"You get to put off going back until I'm done researching all I can about this mysterious tower room tenant."

I put my hands on my hips and rolled my eyes for the fiftieth time today. Cate flashed an all-too-innocent smile at me. "Well," she said, "I'm going to change. I've got my work cut out for me today!"

"I'd say good luck, but I'm hoping you find nothing."

"You should know me better than that. I'll keep digging until I do."

"Yeah," I said with a chuckle, "I know you will. So, I'll have to hope you're forced to dig forever so I can stay in my favorite time period: my own. See you tomorrow, Cate."

"See you tomorrow, Jack. Enjoy the rest of your day off," Cate said.

I made my way to the closet entrance when Cate added, "Oh, and Jack?"

"Yeah?" I asked as I spun to face her.

"Thanks for your help."

"No problem, lassie, no problem," I said.

I made my way down the hall to the main staircase. As I descended it, I became aware that my legs still felt like jelly. My throat began to go dry as my brain grappled with the magnitude of what had just occurred. We had just time traveled to 1856 and spotted a man who had lived over a century before us.

I paused for a moment in the foyer, wondering if I could drive home. How was Cate handling this all so well? She flitted out of the room and off to her bedroom as though she'd just taken a walk around a park. Perhaps she was made of tougher stuff than me.

I caught a glimpse of myself in the large mirror near the front door. I shook my head at my reflection and straightened my shoulders. If the little lassie could endure it, so could I. I gave myself a nod before I pulled the door open and headed home.

The promise of comfortable clothes nudged me to drive a

little faster. I changed as quickly as humanly possible before settling down into my comfortable armchair. I felt exhausted. Like I'd been run over by a train. After twenty minutes, I grabbed my laptop to detail the event in this journal.

I'm still not quite sure what to think about it. The enormity of the situation still escapes me. A little over an hour ago, I nearly came face to face with a living, breathing version of someone who lived over a century before me.

On top of that, Cate's assessment, while annoying, proved correct. The mystery did deepen. Randolph did keep someone in that tower room. At least it certainly appeared so. Was it a girl like the town gossips suggested? Or was there something else going on? Is this the reason he killed someone?

One question is now burned into my mind: what was Randolph MacKenzie doing in that tower room?

CHAPTER 4

September 30
6:27 p.m.

This fine Monday morning brought a welcome respite from time traveling. On Monday mornings, Lady Cate joined us for breakfast in the servants' hall, part of a bargain she made with Mrs. Fraser when she first arrived at the castle. Everyone enjoyed it, even Mrs. Fraser, who had been the staunchest opponent.

The conversation centered around the upcoming party. Mr. Fraser presented Cate with an illustration of an idea he had for transforming the back gardens off the ballroom. I'll admit, his plan was both bold and awe-inspiring. We had our work cut out for us if Mrs. Campbell, the party czar, as I call her, approved it. But if we pulled it off, it would be quite the attraction at the party.

As I headed onto the property for some maintenance work, my mind moved from party details to the mystery that loomed over us from another party over a century ago. Odd, the parallels, I reflected. Here we are planning a Halloween ball on the estate over one hundred years after a murder occurred at a similar party. I wondered if Lady Cate would find out any information. Part of me hoped she did, and part of me hoped she didn't. I still wasn't certain how I felt about time travel.

I'd get my answer later that afternoon. As I watered a few plants in the mid-afternoon, Riley raced to me with Cate following behind.

"Well, hello there, little Riley!" I greeted him. I noted Cate's odd accessories. What had she been up to? "My, my, Lady Cate, this is a new look for you!"

"Huh?" she murmured.

I pulled a few cobwebs from her hair. "Are you trying out your 'Ghosts of the Past' look?" I inquired, referencing the name the party czar had given the upcoming Halloween ball.

"Oh," Cate answered as she swatted away any remaining cobwebs. "I got a little dirty on my latest research mission."

"And where were we researching, Indiana Jones? The depths of a tomb?"

"No, the depths of the tower room," Cate answered.

"Find anything interesting? Maybe a signed confession from Randolph?" I almost hoped she found something definitive. I still wasn't sure about time traveling. Yet a part of me wondered if there'd be a new, interesting piece to the mystery.

"I did! But it wasn't a signed confession."

"Oh, no, let me guess. It's something that deepens the mystery and means your hellbent on time traveling to find out more."

"It's like your psychic, Jack. Has anyone tested you for ESP?"

"I think my sixth sense is about as strong as your comedy routine," I replied.

Cate grimaced at me. "Okay, all joking aside, I found a

note hidden in a secret compartment of the wardrobe accompanied by a drawing. The sketch is of Randolph and the note is addressed to 'R.' The writer apologizes to 'R,' saying the family has endured too high a cost already and would never forget what he had done."

"Who signed it?" I inquired.

"I'm not sure, it just says 'S.'"

"S?" I questioned. "Like the letter?"

"Yes, just the letter 'S.' I'll show you the note and sketch tomorrow after lunch if you have a quick second. It's quite something."

"I'll reserve my judgment for after I see it."

"Fair enough! Well, I think this is a great find, I'm encouraged. I'll let you get back to your watering though, and we can discuss it more after you've scrutinized it."

"Okay, Cate. But don't get too optimistic, you know I'm a killjoy for time travel."

Cate laughed as she began walking away, calling Riley to come with her. "Oh, yes, I know," she said, turning around to wave before she left.

Now, don't tell Lady Cate, but I'm intrigued to see this note. Cate, of course, is reading into every detail with the hopes that it leads us further into the mystery and gives us more reason to time travel. I am a bit more skeptical, but I must admit, piecing this together may be entertaining!

CHAPTER 5

October 1
7:34 p.m.

I headed to the library after lunch to read the note Lady Cate found. "M'lady," I greeted her with an extravagant bow.

Cate laughed and shook her head at me. "Always so dramatic," she teased.

"Always," I said with a grin. "So, where's this letter?" I hoped I didn't sound too eager, but I was interested in reading it.

"It's more of a note than a letter," Cate said as she grabbed a few papers from her desk and handed them off to me.

I glanced at the drawing first. Drawn by a talented artist, the pencil sketch recreated the face of the man we spotted yesterday, Randolph MacKenzie. I shuffled the papers to the note and read it. In scrawled penmanship it said:

R –

I am sorry, but I must go. Your family has already paid too heavy a cost. I will never forget what you have done.

*   – S*

"Well?" Cate asked after a moment.

"Well, nothing," I answered. Cate's assessment was correct. The note gave precious few details, making it impossible to glean any sort of information from it.

"Nothing?" Cate asked, her confusion apparent.

"Yeah, nothing," I answered. "It looks like 'S' vanished and that was that. Seems like 'R' never found the note. He, assuming it's a he, probably wondered what happened to her, assuming it's a her."

"Assuming?" Cate said with a scowl. "'R' has got to be Randolph! 'S' drew his picture and put it with the note, so I think it's a safe bet."

Point taken, I reflected. "Okay, so 'S' left Randolph a note he never found."

"And 'S' must not have been a prisoner. It looks like he or she left of their own free will after apologizing. So, the rumors about a person held captive in the tower room must be false."

I wasn't convinced. The last line sounded ambiguous like it could mean Randolph was a terrible person or a savior. I had to point that out.

"I think you're jumping to conclusions, Cate."

Cate scowled at me again. "If I am, it's not that far of a leap."

"We aren't sure 'S' isn't a prisoner. Look here: 'I'll never forget what you've done.' That sounds ominous to me."

"No," Cate disagreed. "It's like 'you're so great, I'll never forget what you did for me!'"

"Or 'wow, you're a jerk, I'll never forget what you did TO me,'" I countered.

"What about the apology? And the stuff about the high cost for the family?" Cate argued back.

"Perhaps 'S' means the high cost because he's a jerk. I'm not sure, but I don't assume it means Randolph isn't a murderer."

"Okay, point taken," Cate ceded. "Perhaps he is a murderer, but who is 'S?' And what happened there? And why did 'S' leave? There are so many questions."

The lassie was right. This didn't provide us with a smoking gun, but also didn't clear Randolph's name. It only added more questions than answers. That is, if it was related to the situation at all. Though given the drawing's subject was Randolph, I agreed the note related to him. Unfortunately, that's all the further my conjecture could take me.

"And I don't have any answers," I said with a shrug as I handed the papers back to Cate.

"No, I don't expect that you do but..." Cate said. She had that mischievous glimmer in her eye that meant trouble for me.

Out of habit, I shook my head. I was about to hear something I imagined I'd hate.

"We could find the answers." And there it was. The thing I didn't want to hear.

With a sigh, I answered, "I'm not going to argue with you."

"Because you want answers, too!" Cate exclaimed.

"No, because I'll lose again. So, what is your plan?" Okay, okay, so I wanted answers, too. Though Cate was still far more comfortable with time traveling to get them than I was.

"I'm not sure. I have to consider it more. Give me a couple of days to come up with a plan for you to hate."

"Deal. You come up with the plan, I'll hate it," I promised.

Cate smiled at me and nodded her head. "For now," I said,

"I'll hate the idea that you're coming up with the plan at all while I go find these banners with Mr. Fraser."

We said our goodbyes after Cate asked if I had anything to pass along to the dreaded party czar. Thankfully, I didn't. The more removed from that situation for me, the better. I tell you, I think I like time traveling better than I like parties.

CHAPTER 6

October 3
8:03 p.m.

ell, I didn't write yesterday since I had a nice quiet day in my own time period. And I enjoyed every moment of it, too. The only damper was Mrs. Campbell's presence on the estate. I, personally, am firmly in Mrs. Fraser's encampment regarding sentiments toward that woman. I do not like her. She's a bit too pushy for her own good, and poor Cate gets dragged down with her. The lassie really has no ability to say no (other than to me when I suggest we don't time travel!).

Earlier this morning, Mr. Fraser revealed the sketch for his final design for the gardens. WOW, he's got some imagination! It'll take some doing, but it will look fantastic when we're done. Cate's prepared to help along with her party guests. Both Ms. Pearson and Mr. Smythe will be joining us on the estate for the event. And Cate even has an American friend coming across the pond, a co-worker from her professor days called Molly.

Mr. Fraser, Cate and I discussed the finer details of Mr. Fraser's design in the back garden following breakfast. When we'd settled on all aspects, Cate noticed Riley had gone missing. Apparently disappearing was a trick Riley was becoming well acquainted with of late. I offered to help her search.

Cate suggested he'd be near the folly, noting she'd found him there a few times before. We started down the path and sure enough, the little laddie came bounding from that direction. After finding him, I excused myself to help Mr. Fraser with some measurements for his design, but Cate wasn't about to let me get away that easily.

"I was hoping to have a few more moments of your time to discuss something."

Uh-oh, here it comes. "Did you have a question about the party?" I asked.

"No," Cate admitted.

"Did you want me to grab your hundredth order of fish and chips from the pub for you?" I tried.

This comment earned a chuckle from Cate, but she still answered no.

"Oh, I've got it! You wanted to ask me what my costume was!"

"Well," Cate began, "it does involve a costume of sorts, so you're getting warmer."

"Are you having a private costume party that you'd like to discuss?"

"That's one way of putting it, yes."

"And when is this party occurring?" I inquired. My psychic abilities predicted 1856.

"In 1856?" Cate answered, phrasing her response like a question.

Time travel, I suspected as much. I scrunched my nose at her. "I was afraid that would be your answer."

"I have a low-risk plan to get us more information. Not

tons of information, but some! Not even you can object to this one, Jack!"

I bet I could, I thought. "Try me, lassie."

Cate rolled her eyes at me. "It's simple. We travel back when the family is having dinner. We make sure ALL of them are accounted for, then we check the tower room."

Not the worst plan ever, but it still made me uncomfortable. "Oh, that's it, huh? Just go back at night, mosey to the tower room and check if someone is in there, doing what, sleeping?"

"We can check for a light shining under the door!"

"Hmm, we can avoid everyone. This might be one of your better terrible plans, Cate."

"See! I told you! So, when should we go?"

I rubbed my chin in a dramatic display of thinking. As much as these questions intrigued me, time traveling was still not my favorite pastime. "Hmm…" I paused. "Let's see. How about…" I paused again for dramatic effect. "The fifteenth of never? Does that work for you?"

"You're hilarious, Jack. Now, seriously, we should go this coming week, before we get busy with the party. How about this Sunday again?"

"Oh, Cate," I said with a sigh, "you are a handful."

"Is that a yes?"

"It's a reluctant yes."

Cate grinned at me. "Okay, it's a plan! And NOW you can collect those measurements."

"Yes, measurements, a nice, safe idea that won't ruin the course of history, my favorite! M'lady," I said giving her a bow before I returned to the garden as she continued on her way toward the loch.

So, now I have ANOTHER trip to the past to dread. In three short days, I'll take my life in my hands again. I can't shake the feeling that something will go dreadfully wrong with one of these trips. Like we'll erase some vital part of history. Or we'll become stuck in the past. Or when we return, our bodies will be scrambled.

Well, I have three days to fret about it. Perhaps in that time, Lady Cate will change her mind. I doubt it, but miracles do happen.

CHAPTER 7

October 6
9:23 a.m.

Today's the day. Or rather, tonight's the night. I'll be on pins and needles all day waiting for this trip. At least I don't have to change here and drive to the castle in those uncomfortable clothes. Cate suggested I leave them in the bedroom and change there whenever we traveled. I hate the way she prepared for time travel as though it were a trip to the park, but I'll admit this is much easier and minimizes the time I wear that uncomfortable get up, so I agreed. Only a few more hours to wait. I wonder what we'll find…

9:06 p.m.

When I arrived at the castle for the trip, Riley bounded toward me from the loch's direction.

"Hello, Sir Riley!" I exclaimed as the laddie rushed toward me. I caught Riley mid-leap, pulling him close to my chest and rubbing his belly. He was doing well with the new trick I taught him.

"Perfect timing!" Cate called, still a distance away.

"I'm not sure anything about this is perfect," I answered as Cate closed the gap.

"Stop being a stick in the mud! This will be a quick one, just your style. Oh, by the way, I figured out why we may have run into Randolph."

"Oh?" I asked.

"Yes, we traveled back on a Sunday in our time, but in 1856 the twenty-ninth of September was a Monday," she explained.

"Ohhhh," I said, realization dawning on me, "the days of the week are different! Good catch, Lady Cate."

Cate beamed at me. "Thanks. Ready to go?"

"I'm with Gertrude on this one, I'm not a fan."

Cate rolled her eyes at me. "Well, we might as well head in and get ready, it'll be dark soon."

I handed her Riley so she could leave him in her bedroom suite while we conducted our business. "Clothes in the bedroom as usual?" I asked.

"Yep! Meet you there after I've changed and settled Riley."

I climbed the stairs and navigated to the bedroom. Already my stomach churned, and my heart pounded. I should have brought antacids with me. With Cate at the helm, I should buy stock in them, I figure.

I pulled on the old-fashioned clothing. My muscles tensed as I slipped the jacket on and buttoned it. Was it the uncomfortable clothing or my discomfort with time travel making me stiff? Both, I decided.

I opened the door for Cate, then spent the rest of the time pacing the floor. What took her so long? I wanted to get this over with!

Within minutes, my collar choked me. I fiddled with it as Cate appeared at the door.

"I wish we could travel to an era with more comfortable clothing," I said, continuing to fiddle with the stiff material.

"I'm sure I can make that happen," Cate assured me.

I rolled my eyes at her. "Very funny, Cate."

Cate grinned at me. "Ready?"

"As I'll ever be."

We entered the closet and activated the timepiece, landing safely (more or less) back in 1856.

"Looks like we made it," Cate whispered. "Let's go!"

"Agree, let's get this over with. Straight to the tower room and back, right?"

"More or less."

"Caaaaaaaate," I chided.

Cate cut me off before I could complain further. "Come on!" She bounded to the closet door, cracking it open an inch to peer out. "All clear!" she called, pulling the door open all the way and making her way to the bedroom door.

"Wait up," I mumbled, racing after her.

Cate eased the door open and peered out. "Coast's clear, let's make a run for the stairway!"

"Okay, on three," I said before starting my count. We dashed down the hall to the stairs. I beat Cate to it. It appeared her dress made her flight more of a slow lumber. We made it unscathed and began to climb the circular staircase.

The tower room door came into view as we rounded nearer to the top. A glow emanated from beneath the closed door.

"Look!" Cate breathed as she pointed toward the door.

"I see it," I whispered with a nod. "Point proven. Now let's go."

"Just a second. We can't tell what's happening in there," Cate said.

"Nope, and unless you brought your x-ray vision goggles, we will never know."

"I didn't but…"

Oh no, my brain groaned. What hare-brained scheme did Cate have in mind? "Cate, let's just go."

"Just listen!" Cate entreated. "This stairwell goes to the ground level. We could take a quick peek from outside. See if we spot anything."

"No," I argued. "No, absolutely not."

"Okay, you stay here, I'll go."

"Cate! I can't do that!" I countered.

"Looks like you're going with me then," Cate said with a smile. "The longer we spend arguing about it, the longer we're here."

"Oh, Cate," I said with an eye roll. "I hope you don't come across any more mysteries. Let's go."

We descended the stairs to the ground level. My heart thudded in my chest with every step. Every moment we hung around here was a smidge closer to being caught. My head remained on a swivel as I scanned every nook and cranny for another person.

We pushed through the door into the night air without being seen. I could almost breathe a sigh of relief, but we still had to sneak back in and all the way to the bedroom to get back. I swallowed hard, gulping the refreshing evening air to steady my nerves.

Cate scrambled to the area where the tower was visible. I followed her, and we turned to glance at the tower windows. Black nothingness stared back at us. Cate's brow furrowed, and she moved to another position. She glanced at me, a puzzled expression on her face.

"We just saw the lights!"

"Maybe the person left," I suggested. "Perhaps there isn't anyone living in the tower room."

"What are the odds in the few minutes it took us to walk here the person left?" Cate asked.

I was about to give my expert opinion when Cate added, "It's low, I promise."

"Well, it's dark now, Cate," I said.

Cate stared at the tower again. "Or are the windows blacked out? So, no one could see light?"

That seemed like a stretch. "Oh, come on," I started, "how…"

"Jack, look!" Cate interrupted. She pointed at the tower. I followed her finger and saw a flash of light. A warm, yellow glow gleamed from within the tower.

"I knew it!" Cate said, clapping her hands. "Blackout curtains to make it appear that no one is there!"

As always, Cate's assessment proved correct. Someone was in the tower room and the windows were treated so that no one from the outside would be any the wiser. Not just any someone, either. The silhouette of a woman appeared in the window. After a moment, she let the drape fall across the window, hiding her again from sight.

Panic grew in me. We'd gotten what we came for. Every moment longer we spent here increased the probability that we could be caught. "We should go," I suggested.

Cate didn't argue, she must have heard the urgency in my voice. We crept into the castle and through the halls to the bedroom. By the grace of God and sheer luck, we ran into no one. We closed ourselves in the closet and sped the watch, returning us back to our time period.

The moment the timepiece finished its cycle, I loosened my collar and blew out a sigh of relief.

"So," Cate blurted, "there IS someone in the tower room. A woman, not just someone, a woman! And they are trying to hide her presence. That HAS to mean something. But who is it? Why is she there? She must be the mysterious 'S' from the note. Randolph was hiding her in the tower. But why? If he was madly in love with Victoria, why did he bring her?"

My mind spun as it struggled to keep up with Cate's analysis. "Cate, slow down. My heart is still returning to normal speed. I can't keep up with all your questions!"

Cate paced the floor and responded as though she hadn't even heard me. "They are definitely hiding her. But for what reason?"

I didn't know the answers to any of this. My mind reeled, and I offered no response. Cate spun to face me; her face full of excitement. "Are you thinking what I'm thinking?"

"Somehow I doubt it," I answered.

"We need more information!" she said, her eyes growing wide. "We need to go back."

I covered my face with my hands. Somehow I figured we weren't on the same wavelength. I was beginning to wonder if we were still on the same planet. "Oh, Cate, I somehow figured we weren't thinking the same thing."

"Really?" Cate asked with shock apparent in her voice. "How are you NOT thinking that?"

"Go back? Nope, definitely wasn't thinking that, Cate," I admitted. Time travel was not on the top of my to-do list no matter what situation I was in. "I hate going at all, let alone going back to a time when a man is about to commit murder to continue to hide a secret woman in the tower room."

"So, you do imagine there's more to the story, and it somehow involves the mysterious 'S!'"

My eyes went wide. She HAD to be kidding. Out of everything I said, THAT was what she got from it? "Oh, Cate," I said with a sigh, "you always know just how to twist what I say to support you." I laughed. Her ability was almost comical. "You're one amusing lassie. When you're not dragging me back to a time when I have to wear a ruffled collar and almost get killed, that is."

Cate rolled her eyes at me. "You're so dramatic. We weren't almost killed."

"I was so almost killed!" I argued. "By my heart, when it almost attacked me."

Cate rolled her eyes again but giggled at my poor joke. "Oh, stop. Be serious, we need a plan. Hmm, when can we go again? We need a plan that allows us to investigate and perhaps talk to a few people. I realize the party is coming up and you'll be busy getting things ready, but I'd like to eke some time out this week."

"Whoa, whoa, Cate. Slow down."

"Oh, please don't tell me you're not willing to investigate this! We learned way more than we knew when we first started! And even then you determined it was worth looking into! Now we confirmed the existence of a mystery woman and suspect there may be more to the murder than the story from the articles. We need to press on!"

"Oh, Cate," I said with a sigh.

Cate's shoulders sagged. "It's my family. They're important to me. I realize I didn't know them, but I have no other family. The ghosts of my past are all I have."

I eyed the woman in front of me. The lassie had no one outside of little Sir Riley. With both her parents dead, no siblings and no other known relatives, finding Dunhaven Castle was the closest thing she had to finding her family. The promise of helping someone, however far removed on the family tree, must have been more than tempting.

"You're lucky I like you, Cate," I answered.

Cate clasped her hands together under her chin, a smile spreading across her face. "So, you'll go with me?"

"Yes. You'll just go without me and I don't want that. BUT we only go with a plan I like. And we won't just talk to random people. And we're definitely not going to tell Randolph anything we know. We're going to leave the past as intact as we can."

"Deal!" Cate said. "How's Wednesday?"

"As good as any day I guess."

"That gives us time to formulate a plan and make at least two trips before…"

"AT LEAST TWO?!" I burst. "Now wait just a minute…"

"Possibly two," Cate interrupted, "if we find out something that needs to be followed up on. With our party coming up we'll be busy with that and won't have time to travel back. And we're running out of time."

"Time," I reflected, "the one thing we have plenty of."

"We don't! The murder occurs on Halloween! And we'll lose a whole week for the party if not more!" Cate lamented.

"I'm now very excited for the party!" I said.

Cate swatted at my arm. "All right, funny guy. Well, I guess I'll let you off the hook for now. I'll come up with a plan and we can reconvene tomorrow to discuss it."

I wiped my brow. "Whew, sounds good to me. I'm going home to enjoy my modern life."

Cate left me to change into my regular clothes and I headed home for the night. Despite it being late, I wanted to record what happened here before I forgot any of the details.

Obviously, someone was hidden in the tower room. A woman, that is. A woman was hidden in the tower room. Cate's questions made sense. I hadn't read the love letters written to Victoria from Randolph, but I trusted they were every bit as romantic as Cate suggested. If Randolph loved Victoria that much, would he have brought a woman? Though if Randolph loved Victoria that much, perhaps he did kill out of passion.

The more we sought answers, the less things made sense. There was a woman hidden in the tower room. That much we knew. Why she was there and how she got there remained unknown. How she tied into the upcoming murder (if she did) was also unexplained.

As much as I hated to admit it, in order to find any more answers, we needed another trip to the past. In fact, I detested this detail. The next time we had to interact with people. This seemed like a terrible, horrible idea. My mind concocted all sorts of scenarios of what could go wrong. I'm keeping my fingers crossed that nothing does. Looks like I'm on pins and needles again until Wednesday!

CHAPTER 8

October 7
7:17 p.m.

Today consisted of trimming more bushes for the most part. It seems whenever I trim bushes, Lady Cate decides it's a wonderful time to spring a plan on me. I suppose she imagines if I'm working, I'll miss a detail or be more receptive. Either way, Cate caught me trimming bushes in the back garden, readying it for the big upcoming party.

Actually, Sir Riley found me first. We engaged in a lively game of tug-of-war. The little laddie won, of course.

"Well, good morning, Lady Cate," I called as I spotted her in the distance. Riley already tugged against me as he tried to pull the branch free.

"Good morning, Jack," she answered. "Careful, he'll tear your arm off for that prize!"

"Yes, I can see that," I agreed. "A mighty strong little rascal, this one!" I let him pull the branch from my hand. "Okay, you win, big guy!" Riley trotted away, branch in mouth before he settled down to gnaw on it.

"I have our plan all set!" Cate announced as she closed the gap between us.

My stomach somersaulted. I really needed to carry antacids on me at all times. I groaned. "I was hoping for twenty-four hours to recover, at least!"

"Time is of the essence! I spent last night planning, so we weren't delayed!"

I held my hands up in defeat. "Okay, okay. So, tell me this plan of yours?"

"Well, I think you were right." Ah, I reflected, the lassie wanted to butter me up first. "We need to tell Randolph that we are distant cousins, part of the MacKenzie clan. That will give us access to the household and the family. We can use the ruse that we are in the area traveling while you are on business. That gives us an excuse to stay outside of the castle and come and go as we please. Our priority should be learning the lay of the land, having a brief discussion with Randolph and perhaps a few other household members. Just a casual conversation to see what he's like."

"I have so many objections," I began.

"That's perfect," Cate interrupted. "I figured you could imply that you are an attorney."

"Now I have even more objections," I said with a roll of my eyes.

Cate gave me an unimpressed glance. "I promise not to say anything to Randolph that would even give him a hint regarding what we're doing."

"Okay, okay. I must admit, it seems a reasonable plan and a good way to start pursuing this scheme."

Cate grinned at me. "We should go back in the early afternoon, perhaps right after lunch. We don't want to interfere with a meal or preparation for a meal. Since we're seeing Randolph, it shouldn't be too much of an issue since he likely conducts business during this time."

"After lunch on Wednesday, I guess," I agreed. "If we must."

"We must," Cate added with a grin.

So, our plan is set. On Wednesday, we travel back in time to do more than just gawk around. We'll be speaking with real live people who lived on the estate more than a century before us. Again, my thoughts are all over the map. It's astounding, yet frightening at the same time.

CHAPTER 9

October 9
7:54 p.m.

My morning sped by. I dreaded the approaching lunch hour. As I sat down at the kitchen table, I couldn't remember a time in the past when Mrs. Fraser's food seemed so unappealing to me. Cate joined us for lunch. I wondered if she could read my apprehension from across the table.

After lunch, we excused ourselves upstairs under the ruse of estate business, as always. As I changed into the old-fashioned clothing, my mind wandered to our upcoming trip. I blew out a long breath as I steadied my nerves. We'd be fine, I conjectured, as I fastened my shirt and pulled my jacket over it. Piece of cake.

I waited for a few more tense moments until Cate joined me in the bedroom. I almost experienced relief at the sight of her. As anxious as I was about the trip, I was more anxious to get it over with. As the second hand slowed to a crawl, a problem occurred to me.

"I forgot to ask," I whispered, "what's the plan for getting out of here and to the front door?"

"Sneak down the back stairs?" Cate suggested with a shrug.

"As good a plan as any, I suppose." I cracked the closet door open and gave Cate the all-clear. After searching the hallway beyond the bedroom and finding it empty, Cate and I made a dash down the hall, descended the steps and crept out into the fresh air at the bottom.

We circled the castle, careful to avoid being spotted by anyone, and arrived at the front door.

I gave Cate one last chance to back out before we plowed ahead. "You sure you want to do this?" I inquired.

Cate nodded. By the expression she wore, I wondered how certain she was. But I went ahead and lifted the heavy brass lion's head door knocker and let it thud against the plate below. A tense few moments passed before an older gentleman opened the door.

"Yes?" he inquired.

I glanced at Cate for a brief second, uncertain if I could find my voice. She offered an encouraging nod. I returned my gaze to the tall gentleman in front of me. "Jack MacKenzie and wife here to see my cousin, Lord Randolph MacKenzie." My heart thudded in my chest as I told the lie. I expected the door to be slammed in our faces. I was certain my abilities for being untruthful would be detected in an instant.

"If you would be so kind as to follow me, sir, I will show you to where you may wait for Lord MacKenzie," the man announced as he waved us into the foyer.

We followed him into the sitting room. "I shall announce your arrival to Lord MacKenzie at once, sir." With a slight nod, the man departed.

"Great job!" Cate whispered to me once he disappeared from the room.

"Yes, good job, me. I got us into your own house!"

Cate shook her head at me but did not respond. Both of us were far too nervous to continue our conversation. We didn't have long to wait. Within moments, two men appeared. The man who answered the door preceded Randolph MacKenzie into the room.

Randolph dismissed the butler, then approached me. I leapt from my seat on the sofa. I stuck out my hand, suddenly all too aware of my lack of knowledge of any customs from this time period. "Lord MacKenzie," I greeted him, my hand thrust out toward him. "It's a pleasure to meet you, sir. I'm a distant cousin of yours, Jack MacKenzie."

Lie number two. Would Randolph notice the sweat beading on my forehead? Would he immediately realize the falsehoods being thrown at him?

"Jack MacKenzie, I can't say I've heard of you, laddie, but family is always welcome at Dunhaven Castle," Randolph answered. He grabbed my hand in his, giving me a firm and friendly handshake.

Wow, my mind reeled. He hadn't realized the lie I told. Perhaps we'd make it through this unscathed!

"Ah," I stammered, my nerves still on edge. "This, sir, is my wife, Catherine. I sent word ahead through the post of our arrival. It appears you haven't received my letter." Lie after lie after lie. How many before Randolph caught me? Though I made an educated guess that the post in rural Scotland in the 1800s was less than reliable.

"I haven't," Randolph admitted. "The only thing you can count on with the post is that you cannot count on it!"

A smile crossed my face. Randolph played right into my fib, confirming my guess. He approached Cate. She did not stand to greet him. I figured that was customary for this time. Smart lassie. I suppose being a history professor paid off.

Cate extended her hand, palm facing down to him.

"Mrs. MacKenzie, a pleasure."

"Likewise, Lord MacKenzie," Cate responded.

Randolph cocked his head. "Do I detect an American accent, lassie?"

Cate smiled and answered, "You do, Lord MacKenzie. I hail from the other side of the pond."

"I see!" Randolph answered. "Welcome to Scotland, then! And please, call me Randolph. We're all family here." He spun to face me. "Please, please, sit down. Can I offer you a scotch?"

A scotch? My mind whirled. Was it impolite to refuse? Did people in this era drink in the mid-afternoon? Would Randolph assume me a drunkard if I accepted? I sat next to Cate and shot her a glance. She gave a discreet nod.

"How kind of you," I answered, taking her gesture to mean I should agree.

Randolph poured two glasses of scotch. "Anything for the lady?"

"No, thank you," Cate declined.

"Don't tell me you're a teetotaler, Mrs. MacKenzie," Randolph said with a loud laugh as he handed a glass to me.

Randolph sank to his chair across from us. "No," Cate answered, "but I typically only enjoy those beverages at a much later hour."

The answer sufficed and Randolph turned his attention to me. I swallowed hard as his gaze fell on me. "What brings you to my fair land, cousin Jack?"

"Well, as I explained in my letter, I am in the area on some business. I hoped that I could meet some family while here. I apologize again for arriving unannounced."

"Bah," Randolph burst, waving his hand at me. "Nothing to worry about, cousin! And what is your business?"

"I am an attorney, mainly land dealings and holdings." I swallowed a large gulp of scotch after that lie.

"I see. Interesting. And you'll be staying on with us at Dunhaven Castle?" Randolph inquired.

Good thing the burning liquid already reached my stomach, otherwise I'd have choked on it. I glanced to Cate before stammering out, "Eh, no, sir."

"We've taken a place of our own, on the outskirts of town," Cate explained. "With Jack's extended business here, we considered it best to set up our own household." Damn, the lassie was good. If I didn't already realize it was a lie, I'd have believed her!

"Nonsense!" Randolph scoffed. "You're family! Cancel your contract. You'll stay here. You're an attorney, I'm sure you can find your way out of it!"

A laugh escaped me, half from nervousness and half from his rather entertaining joke about attorneys. "While that may be, I am also a man of my word. I'd not cancel a contract out of turn." The first truth I'd told since I arrived here finally surfaced.

"Man of your word, eh? Good man. Honest and independent, just like a MacKenzie." Randolph nodded in approval at me, and I offered him a smile as thanks. "Well, surely you'll dine with us often while you're here, I hope?"

Now, that wasn't going to happen. I opened my mouth to respond, but Cate beat me to it. "How gracious of you, we are delighted to accept your invitation at a time that suits you and your wife, Victoria."

"Perhaps Monday? Victoria is throwing together a little soiree, nothing fancy. I'm certain she'd love to have you attend."

"We are happy to accept," Cate answered. I groaned inside. Why did she have to accept an invitation for dinner?

"Wonderful! I understand the festivities begin at six o'clock. Oh, I'm sure Lady MacKenzie would love to have you for tea, Mrs. MacKenzie. It will be nice for her to have a female friend for tea. I do feel rather sorry for her, moving here to the fringes of civilization."

"We shall plan to arrive at six," Cate responded. "It's such a lovely castle. I'm sure she is contented with such a home despite its remote location."

Randolph smiled at her as he sipped his scotch. "Such a gracious wife you have, cousin. While it's true Lady MacKenzie wants for nothing, her happiness is still vital to me, as I'm sure yours is to my dear cousin."

Cate smiled at him. Now seemed to be a perfect opportunity to escape. "It certainly is!" I finished the final sip of my scotch. "Well, we won't take up any more of your time this afternoon. Thank you for meeting with us and I look forward to dining with you and Lady MacKenzie soon."

Randolph stood as Cate and I did. "Of course." Randolph removed his pocket watch from his vest pocket and checked the time. My mind reeled at the sight of it. Cate carried the exact same timepiece, albeit over one hundred years older, around her neck at this very moment. "Anything for family," he continued. "I shall look forward to seeing you both again."

Randolph crossed the room and pulled a cord. Within moments, the butler returned. "Ah, Thomson, Mr. and Mrs. MacKenzie were just leaving, if you could show them out. And please collect their address so Lady MacKenzie can correspond with Mrs. MacKenzie about an invitation to tea."

"Very good, m'lord," he answered. Randolph left us with Thomson, who guided Cate toward a desk to pen her address. I wondered what Cate wrote as the quill scratched across the paper. Cate folded it and handed the paper to him.

"Thank you, Thomson. We can show ourselves out. We'd hate to trouble you." I recognized Cate's attempt to stay inside the castle in order to reach the bedroom linked to our own time. Clever lassie! A second later, our hopes were dashed.

"It is no trouble at all, Mrs. MacKenzie," he responded, leading us to the foyer. Looks like we'd have to do things the hard way, I reflected. This may prove tricky. My brain already concocted the various scenarios that may occur as we attempted to sneak back into the castle.

We followed Thomson into the foyer. I stared up the main staircase for a moment, wishing we could ascend it and be on our way. As I returned my gaze toward the front door, movement caught my eye. Cate flung her arm across her forehead and fell sideways. She grasped at me in a desperate attempt to stay upright.

"Oh! I feel so faint!" she cried.

"Cate!" I exclaimed as I reached out to catch her. Oh no, I speculated. Some unknown issue affected Cate. Likely linked to time travel, I wondered how serious it may be and if it would prevent us from returning to our time.

"Oh, dear," Thomson murmured. "Is the lady quite all right, sir?"

I didn't know how to answer. I tried to hold myself together. "Perhaps she should lie down?" I needed a moment to deliberate our next move and Cate needed a place to lie down and recover.

"Oh, yes, yes," Cate moaned. "If I could only lie down!"

"Of course, madam. Sir, if you could help the lady up the stairs, I will see to settling her in a bedroom to rest until she has recovered."

I nodded, my stomach turning over as I pondered the situation. I lifted Cate in my arms, struggling to gather the mounds of fabric making up her skirt. We started up the stairs behind Thomson. Cate's head lolled. On the second stair, Cate snapped her head up and offered me a wink. My brow furrowed as realization dawned on me. Cate was faking her illness! A clever ruse designed to get us upstairs!

I followed Thomson through the halls to a bedroom. By luck, it happened to be in the same hallway as the bedroom we needed to reach. Cate's ploy was paying off in spades. I laid Cate on the bed as Thomson hovered in the doorway.

"Shall I call a doctor, sir?"

"No," I responded. I clasped Cate's hand in mine in a dramatic display of a doting husband. "It's likely the journey has been too much for her. I'm sure she only needs a moment to rest and recover, then we will be on our way. Please, don't let us keep you."

"Thank you, sir. I will check back with you in the event that you should need anything or the lady's condition worsens."

"Thank you, Thomson," I said, my focus remaining on Cate.

Thomson's footsteps receded down the hall. When they faded to nothing, Cate popped her eyes wide and shot up to sitting. "Wow!" she exclaimed in a hushed tone. "I can't believe that worked! Hurry! We'll make a run for the bedroom!"

"Best idea I've heard all day," I agreed. We crept to the door and glanced up and down the hallway. I spotted no one. I grabbed Cate's hand, and we hurried down the hall to the bedroom. I wasted no time pulling her into the closet. She threaded the timepiece through the neckline her dress. We both clutched it and activated it to return to our time.

Each of us breathed a sigh of relief. I pressed my hand over my heart.

"I always feel so much better when we're home."

"What an incredible experience, though! My ancestor,

Randolph, right there in front of me! And did you see the watch? He held the same watch that I inherited. It really is mind-blowing," Cate babbled. Excitement filled her voice. I imagined the experience must have been mind-boggling for her.

"That's one way of describing it, I suppose. Clever stunt, by the way. I was becoming concerned about navigating back to this closet without being caught."

"Thank you!" Cate said with a grin.

"And I must admit, that was quite an experience. Randolph seems to be an interesting character, I rather liked him!" I admitted.

"I did, too!" Cate said with another smile. "And now, do you still find it believable that he killed a man because he gave a questionable glance to his wife at the table?"

I considered it. The man seemed affable, polite and well-adjusted. "I suppose it's plausible. He was very family-oriented."

"Oh, come on, Victoria's happiness is vital to him, anything for family, honest and independent, that's what a MacKenzie is! Does he sound like a man who kills someone over a glance, then lies about it?"

"Perhaps he snapped? And maybe guilt got to him?" I suggested.

"He didn't seem like a hothead," Cate replied.

"No, he didn't," I admitted. "He seemed like a right fellow, I felt bad lying to him."

Cate nodded. "A necessary drawback. But consider how much better it will be when we prove his innocence, and he can live a happy life with his wife and child."

"IF we prove his innocence," I corrected. "Now, I better get back to work. I'll leave you to come up with a strategy for Monday. Well, Sunday for us," I said, recalling the different days of the week. "I will be on pins and needles all week."

"Don't worry, I'll have a plan locked down in no time!" Cate beamed at me and winked before she spun to leave the closet.

"Oh, Cate," I said. She glanced back at me. "Before you leave, what did you write on the paper for our address?"

"I didn't," Cate admitted. "I wrote a note stating to leave any correspondence with the postmaster until we had set up our household. I hope that works."

Smart lassie. "Good thinking!" I said. Cate left me alone in the closet. I collapsed on one of the trunks. My mind pondered how Cate took these trips in stride. She almost enjoyed them, it seemed. I, on the other hand, remained on the verge of mental collapse with every journey.

This trip was certainly no different. Even worse, in fact. In this instance, we interacted with people. Real living people. The effects of our interactions could echo through time, creating drastic, unpredictable consequences.

Though our lack of time travel could do the same, my brain suggested. With a sigh, I climbed to my feet. Plenty of work awaited me this afternoon. I could use it to stop my mind from racing through questions that I'd never find answers to. The fact remained: Cate and I were time traveling. We were solving a murder. And it wasn't uninteresting! I'd focus on that.

I left the closet and changed before returning to my hedge trimming. The simple act of shaping shrubs eased my mind, and I pushed the mystery and our unique journey to solve it to the back of my brain.

It only surfaced again when I returned home. As I opened the door, I contemplated recording our experience in this journal. Everything flooded back to me.

What an incredible occasion. I spoke with a man dead long before my birth! Two, actually! But focusing on Randolph in particular, I agreed with Cate's assessment of his personality. Did it fit with that of a killer? In my opinion, no. Particularly when I consider all the facts. The full story suggested Randolph killed a man, covered it up, then later confessed out of guilt.

Perhaps a friendly sort like Randolph could kill in the heat of the moment. Suppose he noticed that longing glance between his beloved Victoria and the ill-fated footman. Perhaps they argued about it. In the heat of the argument, Randolph snapped. He bludgeoned the man to death. In a panic, he created an elaborate story to cover his tracks. But the guilt plagued him. And as the investigation wore on, his guilt ate away at him until he confessed.

A plausible scenario, I believe. But that doesn't explain the alibi. His staff members could have been coerced, of course. Though this scenario involved multiple people lying and not retracting their stories. But still, it could happen. Yes, Randolph COULD have done it.

But I'm not so sure he did. Call it a gut feeling, call it intuition. There's a fifty percent chance Randolph MacKenzie is innocent.

CHAPTER 10

October 10
6:53 p.m.

*O*hhhh, I cannot believe it! I expected to have until Sunday to fret over a trip to the past. Today, Lady Cate sprung a new trip on me. And I agreed!

Cate imagines it may appear suspicious if we don't check for any correspondence in 1856. I must say, I agree. The lassie has thought through everything!

The last thing we need is more suspicion. We already can't explain anything about where we came from. Lucky it's 1856 and not the digital age. But still, Cate's point is valid. We can't go missing for four days then appear for dinner.

So, I agreed to travel back to the past tomorrow morning. Again. At least it'll be early in the morning. I hope not to run into anyone given the early hour. I'll report back when we're safely home! (I hope).

October 11
7:34 p.m.

Mission Correspondence Retrieval complete. We traveled before breakfast. With the time differential, we could easily make it before anyone even knew we were missing! This would mark our fifth trip to the past, but my nerves continued to play up.

Even this short business trip had me tied in knots.

"Just wait until we have to dine with them. This is an easy trip!" Cate kidded when she met me in the bedroom.

I shuddered. "Don't remind me. Okay, let's go check our mail."

Within moments, we activated the timepiece and arrived in the past. We sneaked through the castle and to the outside with no trouble. At this time of the morning, most castle residents were asleep, and the servants were busy readying for the day below stairs.

We circled the castle and headed toward town just as the sun began to rise. The walk to town gave me a new appreciation for modern amenities. The walk itself wasn't taxing, but those clothes added a new layer of discomfort. I can't imagine Cate's trip was much better lugging the massive, hooped skirt. The tough lassie made it look easy, though.

We made it to the postmaster and retrieved our mail. Good thing we checked, a letter awaited us. Well, Cate, specifically. With a letter from Victoria MacKenzie tucked into her dress pocket, we returned to the castle and crept through the halls to the bedroom.

Another trip under our belt. Cate wore an excited grin on her face as she waved the letter around after we returned. I'm curious to know what it says. I'll ask Cate the next time I see her. I hope it doesn't lead to another time travel trip.

CHAPTER 12

October 12
6:07 p.m.

One day away from our dinner date with Victoria and Randolph. I hope to learn something valuable during that dinner party, though I'm not sure we will. Given the long list of dinner etiquette in that era Cate provided me with earlier, I'll be too distracted.

In an effort to be helpful, the historically inclined Countess provided me with information about the finer points of dining in the 1800s. I asked Cate if she could provide a smaller version of the list that I could hide in my hand. The lassie considered it a joke. It wasn't.

I was nervous before, now I'm terrified! To make matters worse, the "rule sheet" indicates Cate and I won't be sitting together. We'll actually be across the table from each other. Apparently, the custom of the day requires married couples to sit across from each other. This means I will have to make conversation with two other people from this time period.

At least that's what the sheet says. I'm to watch the direction Victoria turns after sitting and turn the opposite way and make conversation with the woman seated to my side. When Victoria turns again, I'm also to turn and make conversation with the woman on my other side. What will I talk about to an 1800s woman?

I've got less than twenty-four hours to decide. Though with my inability to sleep, perhaps I can come up with something. I'm certain my mind will come up with one thousand other worries beyond this.

Well, time to go toss and turn. I'll report back after the trip tomorrow!

CHAPTER 13

October 13
10:13 p.m.

As I paced the bedroom floor in my ancient formalwear, I pondered the wisdom behind trying to pass ourselves off not only as relatives of Randolph's but also as honest-to-goodness residents of the year 1856.

I was momentarily distracted when Cate arrived. She looked beautiful. "Wow, that's quite a dress!" I exclaimed as she struggled through the narrow doorway. Her large, hooped skirt barely made it, brushing the edges of the door-jamb as she stepped through. The ruby red of the dress contrasted with the blue of her eyes and her porcelain skin. She'd pulled her chestnut hair into a low bun with a hair comb. It fit her heart-shaped face nicely. I felt a little less concerned. With Cate's elegant beauty, no one would pay one bit of attention to me.

"It is a bit unwieldy, I must admit," Cate answered.

"Please don't fake faint again. I don't think I could navigate holding you in that dress," I said with a laugh.

"I'll have to try another type of subterfuge," Cate replied as she entered the closet.

Go time, I reflected as I followed her. A bead of sweat formed on my brow. "I hope I don't do anything wrong," I muttered.

"You'll be fine, I'm sure! If you do anything that wrong, I'll kick you under the table," Cate said with a grin. I hoped to be deserving of the lassie's confidence as we activated the timepiece.

After a careful search of the hallway outside the bedroom, we crept down the hall and hurried down a set of back stairs to the outside. I breathed a sigh of relief once fresh air entered my lungs. A quick check of the time showed we were too early to present ourselves for dinner. Instead, we opted for a jaunt to the loch. Amazing, I pondered as I gazed out over the calm waters, how little some things changed.

As our appointed time approached, we returned to the castle, and I knocked at the front door. Thomson greeted us, took Cate's cape and showed us to the sitting room. My pulse quickened as he announced us.

"Ah, cousin Jack," Randolph said, "glad you could make it to our little party." Randolph bowed to Cate. "Mrs. MacKenzie, lovely to see you again."

An attractive woman sat across the room on a loveseat. Before our first trip here, Cate informed me Victoria's beauty had been renowned. I assumed, based on her appearance, the woman seated in front of us was Victoria MacKenzie. Pretty, yes, though she didn't hold a candle to Cate.

A smile lit up her face as Randolph introduced us. I mimicked Randolph's greeting to Cate. "Lady MacKenzie, a pleasure to make your acquaintance."

Cate gave a slight curtsy, greeting her in a similar manner.

"Drinks?" Randolph inquired as he approached the bar cart.

I could use one, that's for certain. "I'll have what you're having," I answered as I took a seat across from Victoria. Cate sat next to her.

"I'll have a small sherry," Cate answered. The clever lassie elected to follow Victoria's lead, choosing the same drink.

"I hope you are feeling better, Mrs. MacKenzie," Victoria began.

"Yes, I am, thank you. And please thank Thomson for his hospitality when I took ill. After a few moments of rest, I felt strong enough to travel back home. We weren't able to locate him, so we took our leave, causing no further disruptions."

Victoria nodded. "And I hope you did not find it awkward to arrive earlier than our other guests, but I hoped to spend a small amount of time with family only."

"Not at all, and thank you so very much for extending the private invitation," Cate answered.

"Of course," Victoria responded. "I understand from my husband that you will not be staying with us. I hope the stories of our home haven't put you off."

"Oh, Victoria, please. Let's not start with that!" Randolph said as he handed us our drinks.

"The truth of the matter, Lady MacKenzie, is that we considered it best to establish our own household given that we were unsure how long we may be staying. We did not want to upset your household if our plans unexpectedly changed."

For being so quiet in our time, Lady Cate could certainly handle herself well. The lassie didn't skip a beat with her conversational skills.

"It's no upset at all, and I understand how important family is to my husband. But if you shan't be staying with us, I do hope you will accept my invitation for afternoon tea?"

"Lady MacKenzie, I accept your gracious invitation."

"Wonderful. I hope you will be a fixture on the property despite not taking up residence here."

"Yes," Randolph added. "Please consider our doors always open to you." Cate nodded to him. My brow furrowed as I noted Randolph staring at Cate. Cate seemed disarmed by his extended gaze for a moment.

They broke their eye contact as Victoria began speaking again. Unfortunately for me, Randolph turned his attention to me then.

"So, cousin Jack, how are land prospects? You work mainly in land dealings, you mentioned."

"Quite good," I answered. "Beautiful property in the entire area."

"Ah, so Dunhaven Castle will be worth a fortune after you're finished, eh?" he joked as he sipped his scotch.

I offered him a nervous chuckle. "Sir, this beautiful property is worth a fortune with or without me."

"You find the property alluring, do you?"

"It is very peaceful and enchanting, yes, sir."

"I've always found it so. I say, if you agree, you may be interested in a small shooting party I'm putting together next month."

"Sounds intriguing," I answered. I sincerely hoped we were not still traveling to 1856 in November.

"I do hope you're still in the area and able to attend. The game is quite good. We'll shoot for pheasant."

I plastered a fake smile on my face and nodded. The arrival of additional guests saved me from a response. Cate and I mingled with the new arrivals, with Randolph and Victoria taking the lead to introduce us.

Thomson announced dinner, and we filed into the dining room. I found myself seated across from Cate as she warned me I would be. Victoria turned to the gentleman on her right.

I followed her lead and made some polite conversation about my profession and how I met Cate. After a short time, I noticed Victoria turn in the opposite direction. Everyone at the table followed suit, and I found myself faced with a similar conversation with the woman to my right.

As dinner progressed, I observed the servants. Which one was the ill-fated footman who would soon meet his demise? None of them seemed to pay any particular attention to Victoria. Certainly, none that would warrant being bludgeoned to death. Perhaps Randolph lied about the motive to cover something darker.

Cate and I touched base after dinner. Neither of us noticed anything odd over the course of the meal. Cate suggested we make a quick getaway before the other guests. She would signal me when she felt we could make a polite exit.

We mingled for another thirty minutes before Cate gave me the signal. My heart leapt for joy at being able to escape soon. She announced to Victoria that we would be leaving despite the early hour, claiming she continued to struggle with tiredness after the Highlands journey.

"Leaving?" Randolph inquired.

"Yes, I'm afraid so," I answered. "I'm afraid the journey has been taxing on Mrs. MacKenzie."

"I understand," Randolph responded. "If it isn't too much, I hoped to have a brief word with both of you before you depart."

I glanced to Cate, who offered a slight nod to accept his invitation. I couldn't disagree. I doubted we had another choice. "By all means," I accepted.

"Wonderful, follow me. We can speak uninterrupted in my study. Victoria, please excuse me, I shan't be long."

We followed Randolph from the room. I suspected it wasn't customary for a host to leave his guests, but I hoped I was mistaken. Still, my heart pounded in my chest. It thudded so loud, I worried I wouldn't be able to hear Randolph when he spoke. Randolph led us to his office. I recognized the room, still an office in our time. He poured a drink before taking a position behind his desk.

The uncomfortable silence worried me more. "Well," Randolph began after a sip of his drink, "now that we are alone, I hoped you'd tell me who you really are.

Cate shot me a glance. I stammered before saying, "I'm sorry? I am your cousin, Jack. We aren't closely related. I believe..."

"Yes, yes, I know the cover story," Randolph interrupted, waving his hand at us. "Cousins, distant. A letter was sent but never arrived. You're staying on the outskirts of town, but I inquired after you and no one heard a thing. In a hamlet this size, the arrival of a new MacKenzie would have been the talk of the town, so I have my doubts that your story is true."

"Well, we..." Cate started. "We're not... we didn't..." Cate stumbled around without connecting or finalizing any thoughts.

"Perhaps I'm asking the wrong question," Randolph broke in. "Rather than WHO are you, perhaps I should ask WHEN are you from?"

Cate's eyes fixed on the timepiece poking out of Randolph's pocket before glancing at me.

"I'll take that as an affirmation that my theory was correct," Randolph said. "You are time travelers. Future, I'd say, since neither of you is one of my parents or grandparents."

My throat went dry, and my head spun. Cate recovered faster than I did. "Yes, you are correct."

Ugh, I groaned internally. The situation went from bad to worse. "I'd ask what you're doing here, but I shouldn't know that," Randolph responded. "Well, now that I am aware of the circumstances surrounding your visits, that should make whatever you're here to do easier for you."

"Sorry about lying to you," I said, finding my voice, "but you can imagine the position we're in, I'm sure."

"Absolutely," Randolph agreed.

"Thanks for your understanding. We'll be taking our leave now and returning to our own time. Please enjoy the rest of your evening," I said.

"Oh, before you leave, Catherine, will you still attend tea with my wife?" Randolph inquired.

"Yes," Cate responded.

"Oh, good, I worry about her adjustment to country life. I'm certain it would make her happy."

Cate smiled and nodded to him as we turned to leave. "One more thing," Randolph said. We stopped in our tracks and turned to face him. He studied each of us. What was he thinking, I wondered? Which of us to dispose of first? After an uncomfortable moment, he spoke again. "If you are time travelers, that means one of you is a MacKenzie and one of you is a Reid. I'm going to bet you're the MacKenzie." He pointed to Cate.

"I am! Yes!" Cate responded

"Ah, I knew it. I knew it! She's got the MacKenzie spunk. But, by golly, you're a Yank!"

"She's got a little too much of that in my opinion, sir," I answered with a grin.

"And you've all the practicality of a Reid," Randolph said, addressing me.

"A little too much in my opinion," Cate repeated with a smile.

Randolph returned our expression. "Well, I won't hold you back any further. I'm sure you know the way to the location that will return you to your time. I look forward to seeing you both again and good luck to you in whatever you're attempting to do."

"Thank you," Cate said before we left.

Without another word, we hastened up the main staircase and to the closet. I breathed a sigh of relief as we returned to our time.

"Wow," Cate murmured.

"You aren't kidding," I answered. "How did he figure it out? Are we the worst time travelers ever?"

Cate laughed. "He strikes me as being intelligent. And we had some rather large gaps in our story in retrospect."

"Our second meeting only and he calls us right out. I didn't think I was going to stay upright."

"Silver lining, we don't have to sneak around as much. Now he knows, I get the impression he realizes we're there for a reason and that if push comes to shove, he'd cover for us."

"Yeah, I'm not sure I want to push our luck on that."

"Me either, I agree we should continue to be careful, but at least some pressure is off."

"I could use some of your optimism, Cate."

"Or my spunk!" she said with a laugh.

"You have that to spare, lassie. Oh, I can't believe we have to do this again in two days."

"Hey, you've got it easy! You just have to stay hidden. I have all the hard work."

"Speaking of hard work, did you notice anything out of the ordinary during the dinner?"

"I didn't. If there is an affair, it's well hidden. Although, I don't believe that story. I'm not sure which servant it was from the men that were serving tonight, but I didn't see anything suspicious."

"Neither did I. It would be helpful if we could identify the servant."

"I agree. It doesn't help that there will be no pictures of him. We only have his name. Our best bet is to continue to travel back and spend time in the household and hope to identify him by his name."

I scowled. "Not what I wanted to hear. But I agree."

"We're almost halfway through the month, leaving us only two-and-a-half weeks to get more information. It doesn't help that in less than a week we'll be tethered to our time for a week."

"I can't say that I'm upset being tethered here as you put it. But we'll do what we can before your guests arrive and after."

"Thanks, Jack. I think it's time we get out of these clothes."

"I agree. And you're welcome. I'm actually starting to find this interesting. Randolph seems like a good man, I like him. I hope we can help him. I hope you're right about his innocence."

"I'm glad! Now, let's change out of these clothes," Cate said.

"I'll second that."

"Me too. I agree with you on the clothing perspective!"

"Oh, wow! You mean you agree with me on something? I'm flattered!"

She laughed and rolled her eyes at me. "See you tomorrow, Jack."

"See you tomorrow, Cate. I'll let myself out when I've changed into normal clothes."

I changed as fast as I could, glad to shed the old-fashioned dinner clothes and return to my normal twenty-first-century clothes. I hurried out of the castle and to my car. My mind went over and over the details as I drove home. I tried to keep careful track of everything so I could record it all.

After reviewing everything I wrote, I'm becoming more

convinced Cate may be correct. When we began this process, I agreed there may be something to Cate's theory that Randolph is innocent. But in all honesty, I gave it a twenty percent chance at best.

Now, the needle has definitely moved. The chance Randolph is innocent is growing in my mind with every trip. Randolph does not seem the type. And beyond that, no issues existed like the motive given by Randolph. Certainly this close to the murder, there would be something brewing between Victoria and her supposed lover. Instead, I noticed nothing, and neither did Cate.

We're still not sure which footman is the one with his days numbered, but no one paid any special attention to Victoria.

Of course, this still does not rule out the idea that Randolph murdered him for a completely different reason. Perhaps something else prompted the murder, like a business deal gone bad. In particular, an illegal business dealing. One involving a certain woman held captive in the tower room.

Perhaps, the footman learned of the woman's predicament, confronted Randolph and Randolph killed him! It's a plausible theory. But again, this all hinges on Randolph being a man capable of holding a woman prisoner, murdering someone because of it, and covering it up. He doesn't strike me as the type. I'm not usually a bad judge of character, and my gut says he's not a killer. But the evidence says otherwise. Actually, Randolph himself says otherwise.

I guess we'll find out! Don't get me wrong, I'm still anti-time traveling, but this mystery is at least making it more interesting. Cate returns in two days for a tea date with Victoria. Perhaps she'll score some information during that meeting. We need a plan for that trip. I'll give it some thought.

CHAPTER 14

October 14
5:35 a.m.

I've got a plan for tomorrow's trip! I can't believe I'm excited about this. I plan to run it past Cate today. I hope she doesn't get the wrong idea and mistake this for excitement about time traveling. It most certainly is not. But if we're going to do this, we need to be smart about it.

Randolph deduced we were time travelers within two conversations. One of the reasons he pointed to in making the connection was the lack of scuttlebutt in the town about new MacKenzies. I plan to fix that while Cate is having her tea date with Victoria.

I'll make my way into town, check at the postmaster. Perhaps make an appearance at the pub and a few local shops. I'll spread my name around everywhere so no one else gets suspicious. After that task is complete, I'll return to the castle for a quick meeting with Randolph so I'm on-site when Cate is finished, and we can scurry off to our own time with no trouble.

I wonder if Cate will hate this plan as much as I normally hate hers? Cate? Hate a plan involving time travel? Nah. Even I laughed out loud at that one!

CHAPTER 15

October 15
8:27 p.m.

I made it through another time traveling trek! Is it odd to say this is beginning to become routine? Like clockwork (pun intended), Cate and I met in the closet after changing into our usual 1856 duds.

We are also getting darned good at sneaking out of the castle before we waltz back in through the front door. Well, only one of us did that today. The other of us enacted our bold plan to spread gossip throughout the town about the newest MacKenzies.

Cate and I walked around the castle and down the front drive. About halfway down, we parted ways, with Cate returning to the castle and me heading toward town.

I took a deep breath as Cate tottered toward the castle, appearing awkward in all that fabric. If the lassie could navigate this era in those clothes, I could solidify our backstory by making a few appearances in town.

The gravel crunched under my feet as I strode down the drive toward Dunhaven. Crisp October air filled my lungs, and I noted the scent of pine on the brisk, clear breeze. White clouds dotted the blue sky, though the sun shone brightly above me.

For the first time in one of these situations, my heart didn't pound in my chest. My pulse didn't race, and my knees weren't weak. Perhaps it was my interest in seeing Dunhaven over a century earlier. From old photos and artist's renditions, Dunhaven appeared to have changed little over the centuries.

I would find out in about twenty minutes, I reflected as I stepped off the property. Within ten minutes, the town came into sight again. I marched toward it with a determined step. Within another ten minutes, I ambled down the cobblestone street.

Dunhaven's charm surrounded me. While it hadn't changed much in the over one hundred years between now and my time, it seemed so different. Carriages replaced cars, lanterns for streetlamps, a lack of traffic signals of any kind. Yet the church steeple stood in the same place, so did the pub, along with various other buildings I recognized.

The familiarity brought a smile to my face. Perhaps this was why I didn't feel so nervous, perhaps the fellowship I felt with the town extended to even this time.

I ambled down the street to the postmaster's office. As I pushed through the front door, the man behind the desk glanced up and smiled at me. "Ah, Mr. MacKenzie, correct?" he inquired.

"Correct," I answered. "Jack MacKenzie. Any correspondence for me?"

The man shuffled through some mail. "Nothing, sir."

"Thank you," I answered, about to step back through the door.

The postmaster spoke again, halting my departure. "How is Mrs. MacKenzie?"

"Very well, thank you, sir. She is taking tea with her ladyship now, leaving me to run my errands." Tea with her ladyship, I reflected. Was that correct English for Victorian times? I had no idea, but the postmaster didn't seem suspicious.

"Ah," he said, raising his eyebrows, "how very pleasant for her. Will you stay in town long?"

"We've no set plans," I hedged. "Though we hope to stay for a few weeks."

"And Lord MacKenzie is your cousin?"

"Yes, that's correct," I answered, allowing the door to close again behind me.

"Then Ian MacKenzie is your father?"

I swallowed hard. Who the hell was Ian MacKenzie? My mind raced to process the question. Ian must be Randolph's uncle. I shook my head. "No," I responded. "No, we're distant cousins, not first cousins."

His brow furrowed, and I continued. My palms became warm and damp as I continued my explanation. "My grandfather was Douglas' brother."

"Ah, Alistair?" he questioned. I began to nod as he continued. "Or Duncan?"

I offered a nervous chuckle. "Alistair," I replied. "Golly, you seem to know the family as well as I do. Perhaps better!" Golly? Really old man? Where did that come from?

"Isn't much that goes on in the MacKenzie family that the townsfolk don't follow."

I nodded. "Cousin Randolph wasn't exaggerating, then," I quipped with a chuckle.

"Warned you about the lot of us, did he?"

"Something like that." I grinned at him and he matched my expression. "Well, I suppose I better get along."

"Of course, Mr. MacKenzie. And please pass my kindest regards on to your wife."

"I will," I said before pushing through the door and into the cool October air beyond.

I breathed a sigh of relief as I escaped the situation. Well, that should provide the town's gossipmongers with some fodder to discuss. Mission accomplished. Though I would still put a few more appearances in just to be safe.

I strolled down the streets of Dunhaven. I stopped next at the apothecary and purchased, of all things, a bar of soap. The clerk inquired about me being new in town, leading to the typical conversation in which I identified myself as a MacKenzie, further spreading the tale through town.

I finished at the pub with a fine ale. After telling my tale to the barkeep as I sipped my beer, I began my journey back to Dunhaven Castle.

I'd finished my work; laid all the groundwork for the local gossips to spread around. Dunhaven Castle rose high on the hill above the town. I studied the facade, again so different, yet so much the same. I pondered over whether Cate would have any interesting information gleaned from her conversation with Victoria. I wasn't certain when our next trip here would be, but it would be nice to go into that with a tad more information.

The gravel drive crunched under my feet as I stepped onto the property. Two young men worked in the front garden shaping bushes. I smirked at them. Some things never changed. What I wouldn't give to be trimming those bushes, though. In my modern clothes, of course, and with better equipment than they had.

I approached the castle and knocked at the front door. Thomson greeted me and showed me to Randolph's office.

"Ah, cousin Jack," Randolph said as Thomson exited the room. "And how are you on this fine October day?"

"Splendid," I answered.

"Drink?" Randolph offered.

"No," I declined. "I'd better not. I'm here to collect Cate. She must be long finished with tea."

Randolph let out a loud laugh as he poured himself a brandy. "Long finished? Ah, Jack, you've no idea the abilities women possess when it comes to conversation. I dare say they have not yet even left the table!"

I chuckled at his comment. "You may have a point, sir," I conceded.

"Without a doubt." Randolph eyed me as he returned to his desk.

"Sit, Jack, relax for a moment." He motioned to a seat across from his desk.

I sunk into the chair and offered him a nervous grin.

"You're nervous," he said, reading me like a book.

I chuckled again. "A little, sir. These trips... are nerve-wracking," I stuttered.

Randolph smiled at me and nodded his head. "I under-stand. You're a Reid through and through, aren't you?"

I raised my eyebrows at the statement. "Ah..." I murmured.

"You'll have to meet Malcolm on one of these trips of yours. He is forever lecturing me on the dangers of anything and everything." Randolph made a show of rolling his eyes, a tongue-in-cheek expression on his face. "He prefers estate business to any talk of time traveling or anything else he considers a dangerous gambit."

"Sounds like my kind of man," I replied.

"We'll arrange it!"

I nodded to him with a tight smile. "And Cate," Randolph said. "I still cannot get over it. A Yank! I suppose I should not inquire further, though I am curious. How does a Yank come to be Countess of Dunhavenshire? Can women inherit where you're from?"

I nodded my head. "Aye, sir, they can. And it came as a surprise to us, too. But Lady Cate… well, she was a distant cousin of the former owner. Somewhere along the line, her branch moved to the United States. But she is a MacKenzie through and through!"

"Aye, she seems it," Randolph agreed. "Quite the spitfire."

"Don't I know it," I said with a chuckle.

"You two get along quite well," Randolph said with a wink.

I opened my mouth, though I remained unsure what I'd reply when Randolph continued. "Are you really married?"

"No," I answered a bit too quickly. "No, I am only the estate manager."

"Ah, you must spend a great deal of time together. How does your spouse feel about that? I am assuming Catherine is unwed."

"I'm also unwed," I admitted.

Randolph raised his eyebrows at me. "I see. Not yet experiencing the luxury of marital bliss. You have much to look forward to!"

My eyes widened and I let out a laugh. "That's one way of putting it," I joked.

"You don't agree!" Randolph exclaimed. "I assure you, it brightens your days, brings you immeasurable comfort and companionship."

I nodded as I considered his words. "You love your wife very much," I responded as I lifted my eyes to his face to await his reply.

"Undeniably," he assured me. "Victoria is a ray of sunshine in my life. From the moment I laid eyes on her, I realized I must have her at my side. I did not rest until she agreed to become my wife."

"Very romantic," I admitted.

"There is nothing I wouldn't do to ensure her happiness. You'll see, Jack. One day you shall see!" he said with a grin.

I considered my response when Randolph added, "Well, shall we see how the women are getting along?"

"Yes," I agreed and rose from my chair.

We navigated the halls to the tearoom. "Well, have you ladies solved all the world's problems?" Randolph said as he entered the tearoom. I trailed behind him.

"Oh, Randolph!" Victoria chuckled. "We have not, but we have decided that Mr. and Mrs. MacKenzie shall dine with us two days hence and that they shall attend our ball on All Hallows' Eve!"

"Divine! I am so pleased," Randolph answered. "I do hope you'll join us often for dinner at the castle. It's splendid having family nearby."

"As much as our schedule permits and without us wearing out our welcome!" I answered.

"Magnificent!" Randolph answered.

An idea formed in my mind and I acted on impulse. "I had one request if it's not too much to ask."

"Ask away, cousin!" Randolph said.

"I hope you don't view this as ill-mannered, but would it be possible to tour the castle? I would like to see it all."

"Well, certainly, old chap. Shall we do it at the upcoming dinner party?" Randolph clapped me on the back.

"That sounds perfect, yes," I answered. My gambit paid off.

"Then we shall see you in two days forth and shall give you the grand tour of our family's home!

"Well," I began, "I suppose Catherine and I should be on our way."

Cate stood, thanking Victoria for the hospitality. "I'll walk you out," Randolph offered.

"Thank you," I replied. Randolph led us to the foyer.

"I shall leave you here, dear friends. I know not the reason you are here, but if I may say, I hope it keeps you returning to us. I haven't seen such a pleasant and cheerful look on my wife's face in months."

Cate smiled at him. "We plan on it. We'll see you in two days!"

"I bid you both a fond farewell until then," Randolph said. He turned and departed down the hall, not glancing back.

I breathed my customary sigh of relief when we returned to our time.

Cate batted my arm. "Good going getting us the tour of the castle!" she exclaimed.

"Thanks," I said with a grin. "I expected you would appreciate that."

"Let's see how he handles the tower when we tour the castle."

"I'm interested in that, too. He seems like a nice chap. I hope we don't find anything untoward."

Cate snickered. "Did you just say chap?"

"Sorry!" I said with a chuckle. "I guess the past is rubbing off on me."

"Anyway, I can't imagine anything untoward. He seems enamored and very much devoted to his wife. He dotes on her. After talking with him, I'd be shocked if he was the rogue everyone made him out to be."

"Perhaps he's a fantastic actor."

"Perhaps. But he seems so genuine."

"I guess we shall see," I responded.

Cate nodded in agreement. "Well, I'm going to change and get ready for dinner."

"Great plan. We need to devise a plan for the upcoming dinner. Although, this should be an easy one. We're off the hook with Randolph, no other guests to worry about, and I'm starting to get used to the 1800s!"

"Wow! Are you beginning to enjoy this?"

"I wouldn't go that far, Cate," I responded with a laugh.

I considered Cate's statements as I changed from my old-fashioned clothing. No, enjoying the trips to the past was not how I'd put it. Though, I was intrigued. The mystery deepened, as did my ties to the people of 1856. I liked Randolph, I liked Victoria. I did not want them to live through what they were about to experience. I could imagine how deeply this ran for Cate. These were her own ancestors. She was a direct descendent of this man and his wife.

Even as I write this entry, the conversation I shared with Randolph rings in my head. The man loved his wife. Or at least professed as much. I didn't detect any telltale signs of lying when he spoke. No failure to make eye contact, no covering his mouth, no acute changes in breathing. Nothing Google said I'd see if a person lied to me.

Though even if he truly loved Victoria, he could have killed a man because of it. A crime of passion remained on the table. We're inching closer to the murder. Time will tell.

CHAPTER 16

October 17
6:37 p.m.

*B*ack from another time-traveling trip! Cate cleverly excused us from dinner and sent Mr. and Mrs. Fraser home early. That made it easier for us to travel back in time. We dressed and met in the usual spot and slipped back to 1856.

After our typical creep through the castle and around to the front door, Thomson greeted us and showed us into the sitting room.

"Ah, Jack, Catherine, lovely to see you again," Randolph said as he prepared cocktails for us.

"Yes, thank you for joining us this evening," Victoria echoed.

"The pleasure is all ours," I answered. Despite the awkward nature of time travel, I meant it. "And I must confess, we are looking forward to the tour."

"Yes," Cate added in, "I am fascinated by your home. There is nothing comparable in my country."

"Are there no grand homes in America?" Victoria inquired.

"Grand homes, yes. Castles, no," Cate answered.

"My wife is quite taken with your home," I added for dramatic effect.

"Well, then we should start the tour!" Randolph suggested.

"At your convenience, sir," I said.

Randolph motioned for us to follow him from the sitting room. We spent the next hour "touring" Cate's home. Randolph pointed out several features. It amazed me how much the castle remained the same. We traversed the halls upstairs and down. One room Randolph failed to show us: the tower room.

We ended in the sitting room for another cocktail before dinner. I shot a glance to Cate as we took our seats on the sofa. Her eyebrows shot up for a second as she read my mind.

"I noticed a turret while Jack and I walked the grounds. Forgive me, what room was it on our tour?" Cate inquired. She wore an innocent expression, as though she really didn't know.

"Ah, we didn't visit it on the tour, dear Catherine," Randolph answered.

"Oh, what a pity. I hoped to see it," Cate feigned.

Silence filled the room. I had to make an effort to get more information. "I'm afraid my wife has romantic notions about that tower. White knights rescuing princesses and so on."

Randolph roared with laughter. "I'm sorry, cousin Catherine. There are no white knights or princesses. I'm afraid the only thing you'll find in our tower room are chests full of old articles from past generations. I doubt one could even set foot in the room."

Cate shot me another fleeting glance before offering a smile to Randolph. "Well, there is my romantic bubble burst," she yielded.

"I'm so very sorry to have crushed your quixotic concept of our home. I can only hope to make it up to you with our dinner."

As if on cue, Thomson appeared and announced the meal.

"What perfect timing!" Randolph said as he stood.

As we took our seats at the dining room table, Cate said, "Oh, how silly of me, I seem to have left my bag in the sitting room."

"Oh, you mustn't worry, nothing will happen to it," Victoria reassured her. "We will all remember to retrieve it before you depart."

"Oh, thank you. I should like to keep it with me. If it isn't too much trouble, perhaps one of your footmen could retrieve it?"

"Of course," Randolph agreed. He turned to the man nearest to him. "Andrew, retrieve Mrs. MacKenzie's bag."

Andrew. The name of the man who was about to meet his fateful end. I raised my eyebrow at Cate. I studied him as he left the room, wearing a scowl on his face. To be fair, it appeared the scowl was a permanent fixture. Victoria having an affair with this man? I found it hard to fathom.

Over the course of dinner, Victoria invited Cate to visit for tea and a meeting with her dressmaker on Thursday. Cate would need a dress, so I jumped into the conversation to encourage Cate to accept the invitation. The lassie would enjoy it. The only problem with the date was that Cate needed to return on Saturday in our year. I could not travel with her as I'd agreed to drive to Edinburgh and retrieve her friend, Molly, from the train station. The idea didn't sit well with me, however, it couldn't be avoided.

We gleaned few other details during the dinner other

than Victoria's apprehension over the particulars of the upcoming party.

"Well, that was an interesting evening," Cate said as we met in the library after changing.

"Rather enjoyable," I admitted.

"And very informative!"

"Yes," I agreed. "A clever ruse on your part to elicit the name of the servant!"

"Lucky, too," Cate said, "Randolph chose Andrew. And he omitted the tower room from the grand tour! We KNOW it's not full of boxes, we've seen a woman there."

"Yes, I found it interesting how Randolph side-stepped that when you asked about it."

"I wonder why," Cate pondered aloud.

"I don't know. But if he is lying about it, I can't imagine it's for any good reasons."

"I'm afraid I can't argue with you," Cate answered with a sigh. She sounded deflated. No wonder. Randolph lied to us. The first crack in the friendly facade. Would this lie be the beginning of a long line of poor behavior on Randolph's part?

"Perhaps I'll learn something at my fashion show with Victoria on Thursday… well, Saturday. Thank you for the encouragement to accept her."

"Well, you need a dress, I'm sure. Although, I'm not pleased you'll be going on your own."

"I'm rather sorry about it, too," Cate answered. "I was hoping you could have a peek around the place while I enjoyed my fashion show."

"Gee, and here I thought you cared, Cate," I joked, earning a grin from Cate.

"I'll also admit I will miss you. The only times I've traveled alone were by accident! And they were scary!"

"That's because you assumed you were seeing ghosts!" I reminded her.

Cate laughed, despite it being true. "Well, it's a lot more fun this way. But I'm sure I can handle a small shopping trip while you pick up Molly from the train station. Thank you again for offering to get her. I didn't want her driving for hours by herself in a foreign country."

"My pleasure, Cate. Just don't be late from your little shopping excursion! I don't want to explain where you are to anyone!"

"I'll make sure to keep an eye on my time," Cate joked with a wink. "Now, I suppose I should let you get home. We both need rest before the meeting with Mrs. Campbell tomorrow."

"Yes," I replied, "these extra hours in my day are really becoming exhausting. So is Isla Campbell. So, I will bid you adieu, m'lady!" I gave her an extravagant bow as she said goodnight.

As I climbed into my car, I felt fatigue washing over me. With the time ratio of fifteen minutes to one, we could spend a few hours in the past with only minutes passing in the present. Essentially, our twenty-four-hour days were extending well beyond that.

With a yawn, I fired the engine and made the short trip back to my cottage. Despite my weariness, I decided to record this trip before I fell asleep.

We've identified the footman. I'm not certain this helps, but it does mean we can keep better track of him and pay special attention to any circumstances surrounding him. That being said, I witnessed nothing between him and Victoria. And to be honest, I'd be surprised Victoria would engage in an affair with Andrew or even a longing glance. He isn't the most attractive bloke on the block and his personality doesn't make up for anything. I can't imagine he'd be of any interest to Victoria.

On the other hand, Randolph very obviously omitted the tower room. When Cate inquired about it, he lied. He didn't dodge or evade, he outright lied. Why? What was he hiding? Whatever or whoever it was, he was willing to lie about it. Perhaps Randolph was not the amiable chap he pretended to be. If he was willing to lie, what else was he willing to do? Was he willing to kill for it?

CHAPTER 17

October 19
7:56 p.m.

Cate time traveled on her own today. While I'm normally a ball of nerves on these trips, I believe I was worse today realizing she was going alone. I'd volunteered to pick up her American friend, Molly Williams, visiting for a little over a week to attend the Halloween party.

My heart sunk when Victoria suggested today for a visit with her dressmaker. I realized right away Cate would be on her own, but Cate needed a dress for the ball in 1856. With no way around it, I suggested she attend the tea with Victoria and her dressmaker and agreed to let her go alone.

My white-knuckled fingers gripped the steering wheel as I drove to Edinburgh. How was Cate's trip going, I wondered as I glanced at my watch? Did she make it out of the castle and around to the front door without trouble?

Too bad cell phones didn't work in 1856 or she could

have texted me. I would have insisted on it. A Reid's duty was to protect the time traveling MacKenzies. Not even a year into my job, and I already allowed Cate to time travel alone.

I should have stopped her. What if there was a problem? What if she did something foolish like try to find more information and got herself in trouble? What if she didn't make it back? My mind whirled with possibilities and I found myself driving faster, as though that would improve Cate's chances.

The ride back to Dunhaven went faster than the drive to Edinburgh. Cate's friend, Molly, proved to be far more outgoing and gregarious than Cate. She chattered away to me about anything and everything from her life in the United States to her first glimpses of Scotland. From her friendly nature, I took her to be a nice lassie. While it helped pass the time and made the drive more entertaining, my mind kept returning to Cate.

When we arrived at the castle, I found Cate safe and sound. Cate's attention focused on settling and entertaining Molly. Mr. and Mrs. Fraser and I were all staying at the castle for the week to make work easier for everyone. Mrs. Fraser prepared our usual bedrooms, the ones we used when we last stayed in the castle. I headed to my room early with a book and settled in for the night.

From my room, I heard Cate's door close shortly after. She must be retiring early after her long day of time traveling. I grabbed my phone and toggled open the text app. After thumbing open Cate's message, I typed: *Bed already?*

A few minutes passed, and I wondered if Cate had, indeed, gone straight to sleep. My phone chimed, indicating a new text message. I checked my screen to find a message waiting from Cate. *Got your ear pressed to the door?*

I chuckled at the joke as I responded: *Sound travels in this old place. Just wanted to know how your trip went. We didn't have* our usual post-time-travel analysis meeting. I didn't want to disturb your visit earlier.

I stared at the screen as I waited for a response. My fingers tapped against the side of my phone as my impatience built. At last, a message popped up on the display: *It went well! I had a wonderful time with Victoria! Her dress is beautiful, she really is a fashionista.*

I wasn't ready to breathe a sigh of relief yet. *Any trouble along the way? No issues?*

Not a one! You'd be proud. I went straight from the bedroom to the front door without getting caught. And right back as soon as we finished our tea. Oh... except for when I got caught lurking around the tower room...

My stomach dropped. My fingers flew across the virtual keyboard as I typed. *WHAT?! Cate! Are you serious? What happened? Who caught you? Tell me everything.*

Cate answered in seconds. *KIDDING! I did NOT go near the tower room. Straight to tea and right back home!*

My heart returned to normal speed, and I breathed a sigh of relief. *Not funny! Shame on you teasing a wonderful guy like me!*

Cate sent back an emoticon with its tongue sticking out. I replied: *So, did you pick a dress?*

I did! Sapphire blue to go with my skin and eyes, according to Victoria and Madame Bisset. We're all set for the party! I just need to try my dress on Oct. 28! Fingers crossed it fits.

I sent back: *Oh good, I'm so glad we're set for ANOTHER time travel trip. Anyway, I'm sure your dress is very pretty. And I don't want to disturb your night, just wanted to check in!*

Cate's next text message read: *You're not disturbing me, but I am going to turn in early!*

Okay, good night, Cate, sleep well!

Good night, Jack! And thanks for checking in!

I set my phone on the night table and settled back into my pillows. Well, Cate had made it to 1856 and back with no hitches, no problems. AND she didn't even attempt any crazy investigations on her own. With my mind settled, I switched off the light and closed my eyes for a good night's sleep.

CHAPTER 18

October 25
11:43 p.m.

Well, it has been almost a week since I've written. With the Halloween party earlier this evening, it's been all hands on deck for the party preparations. This, coupled with Lady Cate entertaining guests in the castle, has meant we were free of time travel!

That, however, did not stop Cate from investigating the murder. The adventurous lassie wandered to the tower room again last night. Before our lunch, Cate requested my presence. At first, I wondered if it concerned the party preparations. I should have realized it did not.

"Everything okay with the party preparations?" I inquired.

"Yes. It has nothing to do with that. I found something I'd like you to take a glance at."

"Care to give any more explanation?" I questioned.

"Yes, but not just yet," Cate responded. "I want you to look at it first and give me your impression."

Sounded ominous. My mind stretched to find answers to Cate's summons. I followed her to her sitting room. From the side table next to her chaise, she picked up an item enclosed in a plastic bag. She passed it off to me. My arm dropped as I accepted it.

"Wow, it's heavy!" I exclaimed. I spun it in my hands as I studied it. "Something I'm supposed to notice?"

"Turn it over," Cate instructed.

"Oh!" I said as I flipped it. A rust-colored stain covered the bottom. "Is that blood?"

"I'm not sure," Cate answered, "but that's what I thought."

"Where did you find this? And why do you think it's blood? I mean, it looks like blood, but why would there be blood on this paperweight?"

Cate stared at me for a moment before answering. "I found it in the tower room, wedged under the wardrobe. The same one where I found the mysterious note from 'S.'"

My brows knit together, and I scrunched up my face as the realization hit me. "You think this relates to the murder?" I said, phrasing it as a question.

Cate confirmed my suspicion with a nod. "Yes. Well, that's the most obvious idea in my mind."

"Cate, surely the police would have found this when the murder occurred. What are the chances the murder weapon lay hidden in the tower room for over a century?"

"I wondered about that, too. But I re-read the articles about the murder last night and this morning. When the body was first found, they assumed he had died from the fall. They wouldn't have looked for a murder weapon. They would have presumed the fall killed him, whether or not it was an accident. It was only after the autopsy that they realized he was dead before he fell. By the time they searched for the murder weapon, a week had already gone by. They could have easily missed it!"

I considered Cate's analysis. "It's a long shot, but you could be correct. They found he was killed by blunt force trauma to the head, right?"

Cate nodded again. "Yes, that's right. This is the sort of object that may have struck the fatal blow."

"Or it could be rust and discoloration from being stuck under the wardrobe for years," I suggested, giving an alternate explanation.

"I have a method to tell if it's blood," Cate countered.

"I'm all ears."

"We can put a few drops of peroxide on it. If it's blood, it will bubble. If not, it won't!"

"Worth a try, I guess," I answered. "Do you have some?"

"Yes, let me grab it!" I should have known she'd be prepared, I reflected as she disappeared from the room. She returned with a bottle and an eyedropper. "Okay, open that bag, and let's try this!"

I pulled the bag open and withdrew the item as Cate filled the eyedropper with peroxide. I flipped the paperweight and Cate dribbled a few drops onto the stained surface. Within seconds, the peroxide bubbled and fizzed. I glanced at Cate. Blood. She was correct.

"So, it is blood," Cate stated.

"Looks that way," I agreed. "You may be right, Cate. We may have a murder weapon in our hands."

"I'm not sure if that makes me feel better or worse," Cate answered.

"Well, it tells us where the murder occurred, most likely."

"Yes, I'd say it's likely the murder occurred in the tower room. I doubt someone bludgeoned Andrew to death somewhere else, then went to the tower room to hide this object after throwing his body from the window there."

I nodded in agreement. Cate suggested we head to lunch since we'd likely learned all we could from the paperweight.

Today, on the day of the party, Cate was in charge of lunch. I worried we'd be fed a bowl of marshmallow-filled cereal. Instead, Lady Cate ordered a variety of pizzas, which I thoroughly enjoyed!

I didn't have a chance to consider Cate's find until now. After lunch, little Sir Riley did a disappearing act. In a panic, we all helped Cate search for the pup. As it turned out, Riley's vanishing acts of late were a result of him visiting a friend. Riley had found another dog on the property, hiding in the folly. He'd been plying the poor fellow with food and treats.

Cate and I discovered him during our search for Riley. Cate insisted we take him to the castle and clean him up before the party. Little Riley seems enamored with his new pal. I checked on them before the party began. The two pups were curled together in Riley's bed, happy as could be.

As luck would have it, the dog came from Bailey's, a local farm. The owners offered him to Cate, and she instantly accepted. Looks like we have a new member of the family. Cate gave him a fitting name: Bailey.

Outside of that, the party went over well. All guests departed the castle with a large grin and a hearty "thank you" to Lady Cate. Everyone seemed to enjoy themselves, even me. Though, I admit I am glad it's over. I will be happy to remove the decorations, though, from the sounds of it, I think these events may become a regular occurrence on the grounds. Oh well, the castle's beauty can shine and maybe it will limit our time travel, too!

CHAPTER 19

October 28
10:02 p.m.

With all the guests gone as of this morning, our time traveling adventures resumed today. A Tuesday in 1856, Madame Bisset was set to return with a newly tailored dress for Cate. The trip would provide a nice distraction for Cate, I figured. With all the guests gone, the castle would return to the fortress of quietness and solitude Cate enjoyed on a regular basis. However, although Cate loved her no-frills life, I was certain she'd miss her guests.

On a side note, Molly is set to return at the end of the year! Apparently, she detests her life and job in the US and took Cate up on an offer to train under Mrs. Fraser to become the next housekeeper. The lassie couldn't stop babbling about it after she accepted. Will this prevent us from time traveling, I wonder? Probably not, but a guy can hope!

On to the juicy stuff! Cate and I parted ways in the foyer.

Thomson allowed me to find my own way to Randolph's study as he led Cate to Victoria's suite.

I navigated the halls, arriving outside Randolph's office. I rapped on the door with my knuckles.

"Come in!" Randolph's voice hollered from inside.

I pushed the door open further and stepped inside. Randolph sat at the desk, spectacles perched on his nose. Another man hovered over his shoulder. Randolph glanced up over the half-glasses. "Ah, cousin Jack!" he greeted me with a smile. "Come in, come in. Drink?"

I declined as I approached the desk. "Are you certain? I feel this occasion calls for one," he answered.

"Occasion, sir?" I questioned.

"Yes," Randolph said, rising from his seat and crossing the space. He pushed the door shut before he spun to face us. My mouth went dry, and my heart pounded. What was Randolph getting at? I hated surprises. "Jack Reid, meet your ancestor: Malcolm Reid." He motioned to the man standing behind the desk.

I twisted to glance behind me at the man. The brown eyes of my great-great-great-grandfather studied me. I explored his face. A resemblance existed between him and Pap, I reflected. In fact, the case could be made he had a certain resemblance to me. I opened my mouth to speak, but no words came out. I fumbled for another moment, trying to find something to say beyond a childish "hello."

Randolph spoke before either of us. "I do not know the exact nature of your relationship, nor do I need to. Yet, regardless of the closeness or distance of your relationship, this moment is momentous."

"Indeed, it is, sir," I choked out.

Malcolm smiled at me as he stuck out his hand. I accepted it, shaking hands with my great-great-great-grandfather. Odd, my mind pondered, currently at age twenty-four, my great-great-great-grandfather was younger than me. "Good to meet you, Jack," he said with a broad smile and a thick Scottish brogue. "Randolph tells me you hate time traveling."

I broke into a grin. "Indeed, I do!" I said with a hearty laugh.

"Why don't I give you gentlemen some time for a private conversation?" Randolph suggested.

"Oh, that's not necessary, sir," I insisted. "I won't chase you from your own office. Particularly when you are working on business." I motioned toward the paperwork spread across the desk.

Randolph held up a hand as he clutched the doorknob with the other. He shook his head. "Work can wait. Family first." He offered a half-smile and a wink before disappearing through the door behind him.

I faced Malcolm again. He shrugged at me. "You can't talk to a MacKenzie once they've made up their mind," he said with a chuckle. "Shall we sit?"

I eased into the chair behind me as Malcolm rounded the desk and sat in the chair next to me. "Lord MacKenzie… Randolph tells me you're from the future, how interesting," he began.

"Aye," I answered. "So much has changed, yet so much remains the same."

"It's good to know Dunhaven still exists!"

"Aye, she still exists, sir. As lovely a town as she ever was."

"And the Reids persist," he replied with a grin.

I offered a nervous chuckle. "That we do. We're a hearty breed!"

"And a cautious one," Malcolm added. "Randolph told me of your first few encounters and the conversation where you revealed your true identities. He guessed you were a Reid right away due to your pragmatism. It must have some bearing on our survival, I'd wager."

"Ah, yes. I like to call it prudence. Cate likes to call it being a spoilsport."

Malcolm chuckled. "I believe Randolph judges me in the same way. But since the beginning, the Reids have been tasked with tempering the sometimes-overzealous nature of the MacKenzies."

I slouched a bit in my chair, my muscles relaxing as I pondered the statement. "May I ask, sir…"

He held up his hand. "Please, call me Malcolm. We are family, after all."

I smiled at him. "Malcolm," I repeated. "May I ask you, has tempering their rather impertinent nature always been a feat?"

Malcolm threw his head back, a belly laugh escaping him. The laugh proved infectious and I, too, began to chuckle. "Forgive me," Malcolm answered after a moment. "It is nice to discuss this with someone. Not just the sometimes unwieldiness of the MacKenzies but time travel in general."

"They are rather unmanageable, aren't they? As is this time travel thing! I've still not become accustomed to it. My heart pounds every time. Even with Randolph aware, I'm still afraid of doing something wrong."

"Aye, I agree. I always urge caution. Caution, caution, caution. Randolph says I sound like a broken record. Yet, we do not understand the power we hold in our hands."

"You've taken the words right from my mouth," I admitted.

"Power for good, Randolph always counters. But good by whose estimation? The definition of good is subjective. Different for everyone."

"That is an interesting point. I suppose what someone imagines may help the situation might, in fact, do more harm. This lends itself to my largest concern, which is irreparably changing the basic fabric of time. What if we travel to a time before ours and change it so fundamentally that our current world is unrecognizable when we return?"

Malcolm nodded as he considered my point. "Perhaps…" he began before pausing. "Perhaps the universe has a way of correcting itself. Perhaps the choices we make will somehow equalize."

"Perhaps, but what about the paradox of killing your father before he fathers you?"

"Ah, well," Malcolm said, leaning forward toward me, "that is why the basic rules exist."

I rattled off the rules as I remembered them. "You should not travel to a time in which you already existed. You should not revisit a time you've already traveled to because you exist in it. You cannot disappear to another time band for the entirety of your life. Always keep an eye on your time. But none of those prevent that most basic paradox."

"You've forgotten one. Or perhaps it has been lost over the generations."

"Oh?" I inquired.

"You must only use time travel for honorable purposes, never evil."

My brows pinched together. "I've not heard that one. And I don't expect the man who shared this information with me left something so vital out on purpose."

"No, I'm not suggesting your father left it out. It's rather an unwritten rule, though. It may have simply slipped away."

"My grandfather, actually," I corrected. "My father died at a young age."

"Oh, I am sorry, Jack," Malcolm responded, his face screwing up with concern.

I waved it away. "No, please. It's all right. Though I will keep that newfound rule in my mind."

"Our real goal here is to protect this secret," Malcolm continued. "It's never been to suppress it, only to protect it."

"You're beginning to sound like a MacKenzie," I teased.

Malcolm chuckled. "Perhaps, though, it is true. Protect, Jack. Always protect both the secret and the MacKenzie who carries it with you."

"I'll admit, that eases my mind regarding these trips. I remain concerned, of course, but it provides some measure of comfort to me."

"And to be clear, the MacKenzies are far more enthralled with the allure of time travel than I."

"Allure, that's the perfect word to describe it. Cate seems enamored with the entire prospect. Like a giddy child with a new toy."

"It's their nature," Malcolm informed me. "MacKenzies always tend to have this outlook. In some ways, they almost believe they are invincible. That is why it is crucial we temper them and protect them. The sacred pact between Douglas and Jaime. Each of them balanced the other. Jaime's discretion tempering Douglas' enthusiasm and Douglas' verve encouraging Jaime's austerity."

"Wow, that's… profound," I admitted as the words sunk in. It described the relationship between Cate and me well.

"It is a simple truth. Reids and MacKenzies complement each other in perfect balance. Always have and always will. It is… our destiny."

"Destiny. An interesting concept when dealing with time travel."

Silence fell between us for a moment. "Perhaps we could move on to another topic. Something more fun," I suggested.

Malcolm sprang from his chair and hurried around the desk. He snatched a handful of papers and spread them across the desk in front of me. I recognized the layout of the castle on the sketches.

"We are adding indoor water closets! All the rage in places like London, I'm told. Lord and Lady MacKenzie suggested it after a trip there. Not very new, of course, in those parts, but new to us here. What an undertaking! Though it will be well worth it, I imagine."

I stared at the plans, noting the modifications being proposed. A smile spread across my face as I studied them. My mind whirled, considering the adaptations. We spent the next twenty minutes discussing, modifying and bettering the plans.

As we discussed whether a downstairs water closet was a prudent addition, Randolph rejoined us. "Discussing estate business, I see," he assessed as he entered. "Both of you, true Reids through and through."

"Jack has offered some interesting insights on the water closets," Malcolm answered. Malcolm passed along my ideas before he rolled up the plans. "Well, I've got some modifications to make to our plans and budget. I shall have it for you tomorrow."

"Good man," Randolph said, clapping him on the back.

"Well, I hate to cut this short, but I do have some other business I must attend to," Malcolm said to me.

"Of course," I answered. "Believe me, I understand."

"No rush to handle anything, Malcolm," Randolph assured him as he checked the gold timepiece. "Stay, relax."

A few giggles floated down the hall. "That's likely Cate coming now," I answered, absolving Malcolm of any obligation to stay on my behalf.

He smiled at me as though he understood my motives. "I hope to see you again, Jack." He shoved the papers under his arm and stuck out his hand. I grasped it and gave it a hard shake.

"Count on it," I promised.

He ducked out the door as Victoria and Cate entered. Randolph checked his timepiece again. "Are the dresses in order?" he asked as he glanced down at it.

"Exquisite," Victoria promised. "I am so pleased Madame Bisset could provide Catherine with as lovely a dress as mine."

Randolph nodded at Victoria. "Wonderful, dear," he responded.

"The color is simply perfect for Catherine's porcelain skin," Victoria continued. "And a contrast to my red dress. We shall both stand out in our own way."

Randolph clicked the timepiece closed after another check of it. "I am certain of it," he assured Victoria.

"I've offered Catherine the sapphire necklace," Victoria said. "It is a perfect match to her dress. Madame Bisset re-dyed the fabric to ensure it."

"Of course, dear," Randolph replied. "You are an expert in these matters, I trust your judgment as I am certain Catherine does."

"Well, it sounds as though you ladies have everything sorted," I chimed in. "We should be going, dear."

"Yes, I am certain you've much business to attend to, cousin Jack. I, also, must attend to a few matters. If you'll excuse me, I shall leave you to find your own way out. You are, after all, family. No need to stand on pomp and circumstance."

"Of course, Randolph," I answered. "Until next time." We shook hands and Randolph disappeared down the hall. Cate and Victoria said their goodbyes, and Victoria left us outside Randolph's office.

"That was something. Tell you when we get back," I said, referencing my meeting with Malcolm. My mind still spun from it. I stepped toward the foyer and main staircase. Cate tugged my arm, stopping my progress. "What?" I questioned.

"I think we should follow Randolph," she whispered.

"Follow Randolph? Why?" I asked with my voice lowered.

"Didn't you notice how troubled he seemed? Kept

checking his watch. He was distracted. We should follow up on that.

"Perhaps he had something important to do," I countered.

"Or perhaps this ties into the murder. We're days away, and Randolph seems preoccupied. I think we should at least check it out."

"Okay, okay," I acquiesced. "But we cannot, under any circumstances, prevent this murder from happening. I'm not even sure we should help Randolph stay out of jail, but I understand your impulse to protect your family.

We hurried down the hall in the direction Randolph went earlier. From a window, Cate spotted Randolph outside on the path leading to the loch. We followed, keeping a safe distance so we could remain unseen.

We sheltered behind a large tree with the loch visible. Randolph continued down the path toward the water's edge. As he approached the bank, Andrew revealed himself from behind another tree. Cate smacked me in the chest. I rolled my eyes at her. Right again, Cate, right again, I thought.

The two men conversed for a few moments. From their posture and gesturing, they were not engaged in a friendly conversation. After a few moments, Randolph grasped Andrew by the collar. He shook him before tossing him backward. Randolph stormed toward the castle, passing our hiding spot as we shrunk into the shadows of the large tree.

"Now what?" I whispered.

"Let's follow him," Cate said, pointing. I followed her finger. It signaled toward Andrew.

"I was afraid you'd say that," I said. Andrew passed our hiding spot a few moments later. We waited until we could follow while remaining unseen. When we entered the castle, we spotted no one.

"Let's split up," Cate suggested.

"That's a terrible idea, Cate," I admonished.

"We don't have a choice," Cate countered. "I'm not taking no for an answer." She sprinted up the main staircase two steps at a time. It was a comical display as she fought the weight of her domed dress.

I groaned as she scampered away from me, her skirts flurrying around her as she raced upstairs. I stood at the bottom of the stairs for a moment, weighing my options. I considered following her. That would likely end in an argument and result in me returning right back to this floor to search for Andrew.

I decided to do a cursory search of the main floor before following Cate upstairs. I glanced into the sitting room and found it empty. I raced down the hallway, glancing in rooms as I passed them. I found no one.

With a shake of my head, I sprinted back to the main staircase. I took the stairs two at a time, climbing to the second story. I needed to find Cate as soon as possible. I stood on the landing at the top and glanced side to side. Which way, my mind questioned?

A thought crossed my mind, and I raced to the hallway on my left. I wound through the hallways with one destination in mind: the tower room.

As I approached the curving stone staircase, Cate emerged, nearly toppling into me.

"How did I know I'd find you here," I said as I grasped her arms to steady her.

"Ah, Mrs. MacKenzie," a new voice joined in. "I see you have located Mr. MacKenzie. I shall call off the dogs."

Oh, no, I mused, Cate not only visited the tower room, but she also ran into Andrew along the way. My brow furrowed, and I glanced to Cate. "Yes, I ran into Andrew while looking for you," Cate explained. "I'm sorry I lost track of you somewhere."

"Well, you found me!" I played along.

"How fortuitous. Mrs. MacKenzie seems to have an innate ability to lose precious things, then wander about searching for them in places she shouldn't."

Andrew's tone was noticeably acrimonious, bordering on angry. I didn't care for his tone or the manner in which he assumed he could behave toward Cate. "Excuse me?" I questioned him, placing myself between Andrew and Cate.

"Mrs. MacKenzie shouldn't be wandering the halls of the castle, sir," Andrew responded.

"Mrs. MacKenzie and I are family, sir. Lord and Lady MacKenzie have graciously opened their home to us. I do not believe either of them intended it to have the restrictions you are implying."

"You misunderstood me, Mr. MacKenzie," he replied with a smirk. "I am only concerned for your wife's well-being. The castle has many dangerous places, including the tower room, which is filled with many trunks. She may be hurt should one of them fall on her."

Yeah, I bet, buddy, I bet, I ruminated. His warning had little to do with his concern for Cate's well-being. The only danger that existed in the castle for Cate was Andrew himself.

"How kind of you to exhibit such concern for my wife. I will be sure she is cautious in future visits."

Andrew forced another sour smile onto his face and nodded at me as he pushed past us down the hall.

As he rounded the corner into another hallway, Cate suggested we return to our own time.

"Great idea," I agreed.

I waited until we were safely returned to the present before I warned Cate. "Don't do that again."

"Do what?" Cate inquired.

"No splitting up! I don't even want to travel back, yet I know you'll never agree!

"We must go back. Victoria will be crushed if we don't attend the party!" Cate argued.

I rolled my eyes as I sighed. "Yes, yes, I realize that. Randolph made it clear how much Victoria was enjoying your time together. But I think we need to have a serious conversation about dropping this murder investigation, Cate."

"Why?

My eyes went wide at her question. She couldn't be serious! "Cate! Did Andrew not give you the same vibe he gave me? He was threatening us, in particular, you!"

"I don't…" she began.

I interrupted her, waving my arms in the air to signal her to stop. "No, no, no, no, no. I do NOT want to hear you defend him! It was obvious he was threatening you."

"Which only makes me more curious!" Cate countered.

"Bah!" I exclaimed, throwing my arms at her in frustration.

"Think about it!" Cate insisted. "I caught him leaving the tower room. He was attending to whoever is hidden there. Who is it? Why are they hiding her? Why is he privy to the secret? Why was he arguing with Randolph?"

"I don't know the answer to any of those," I admitted. "But given what we witnessed today, it is possible Randolph killed him. You saw the hostility between them firsthand."

Cate remained silent for a moment. "I still disagree," she responded. "Randolph would not have put his family in harm's way by doing that, even if he is prone to losing his temper."

I shook my head at her. "I don't want you alone with that man again."

Cate paused again for a moment. "We should attempt to gather more information in the remaining days we have. Do you have time for a quick trip tomorrow and maybe Wednesday? I'll come up with some excuse to visit."

"Oh, Lady Cate, I will never win. Okay, okay, whatever you say, boss. I'm beginning to look forward to this guy being gone."

"He will be soon enough," Cate reminded me. "That's why we need to gather as much information as we can before he makes his exit."

"Okay, but ONLY because we are already committed to this investigation. And NO splitting up!" I insisted.

"Same time, same place tomorrow," Cate agreed.

"Guess so," I acquiesced.

"Oh, hey, what did you want to tell me when we got home?" Cate inquired.

"Oh!" A smile crossed my face as the happier memory replaced my concern over Andrew. "I had almost forgotten in the excitement. I met my great-great-great-grandfather."

Cate grinned at me. "Malcolm Reid? Was he the man we passed on our way into Randolph's office?"

"None other. That was… strange. I can see the appeal, though. You must feel the same with Randolph and Victoria."

Cate's smile broadened. "Yes, they are my family. I feel a connection to them, no matter how odd that may sound."

"I understand now, Cate. Meeting Malcolm was… staggering, mind-blowing. I now understand your enthusiasm for time travel."

"I'm glad you met him," Cate replied. "I'll bet you'll be seeing more of him."

I wrinkled my nose at the idea of more time travel but smiled despite myself. "Okay, okay, I guess that's a good thing."

We parted ways after that to change and return to normal life. My mind dwelled on the trip as I completed my remaining tasks for the day. Before leaving the estate, I texted Pap about stopping by. The old man agreed as long as I brought him some beer. Funny bugger.

I stopped for a six-pack before popping into Pap's cottage.

"Did you get the local?" he called from the kitchen.

"Aye, your favorite!" I answered.

He ambled into the living room from the kitchen, two mugs clutched in his hand. "Had these ready since you texted," he said as he handed one off to me. "I hoped I didn't have to waste them on some watered-down inky-pinkie."

I guffawed as I sunk into an armchair and cracked open a beer for him. "No bad beer here, Pap. I know you better than that." I poured myself a glass and raised it at him. "And you should know me better than that to think I'd buy you bad beer."

"Aye, that I do, laddie, that I do." He sipped the amber ale. "Oh, that's good." He paused for a moment as he imbibed another sip. "Now, as I was saying, I do know you better than that. Which is why I know you're here for a reason. So, tell me, Jackie, what's on your mind?"

"Can't a fellow buy his grandfather a beer without an ulterior motive?"

"Sure, he can," Pap answered me, "but he didn't."

I shot him an innocent glance and shrugged my shoulders. "Bah, Jackie, I know you better than that like I said. Now out with it. What's on your mind that's got you buying my favorite craft beer on a Monday night?

The old bugger knew me far too well. I sipped my ale again before I admitted he was correct. "All right, all right," I said, holding my hands up in defeat. "I do have an ulterior motive."

Pap raised his eyebrow and smirked at me. I continued, after taking a moment to gather my thoughts. I wasn't sure I could get the words out. A smile crossed my face, and I spoke. "I met Malcolm Reid today."

Pap raised both his eyebrows at me. "Been time traveling, eh, Jackie? And met your great-great-great-grandfather whilst doing it?

"Aye, Cate and I have been time traveling and for the first time today, I met one of our ancestors."

"How d'you find him?"

"Well! It was…" I paused. "Momentous, to say the least. I quite liked him!" Pap offered a half-smile. "Have you met him?" I asked.

"Once, yes," Pap admitted. "I remember I found it odd meeting my grandfather's father."

"Odd doesn't fully capture this," I replied.

"It is quite an experience," Pap agreed.

"I… I couldn't think of anyone else I wanted to share this with except you."

"Outside of Cate and me, there's no one else you can share it with," Pap pointed out before sticking his tongue out.

"Very funny, Pap," I said with a roll of my eyes. "I meant I wanted to share this with someone and who best to understand meeting his ancestor than you."

"Aye, I understand you, Jackie. Certainly, the young lassie will understand, too."

"I'm certain she does. Part of the reason we're time traveling is to help Randolph. After meeting him, she considers him family. She's convinced he's not a murderer and determined to prove it."

"How's it look?" Pap questioned.

I shrugged and sucked in a deep breath.

"You think he's guilty?"

I considered it for a moment. "I did. I do. Maybe," I answered in staccato fashion as my thoughts spilled from my brain to my mouth.

"Care to explain that illogical answer?"

"It's complicated."

"We've got 2 more beers a piece to explain it over," Pap suggested.

"Drinking them all tonight, are we?"

"No sense wasting them or saving them!"

"All right," I agreed. "I'll explain myself." I slid him another bottle. He refilled his glass and settled in for my story.

"When Cate first approached me with this, I'd have put the probability at eighty percent Randolph committed that murder."

"Eighty? Where's your head on the other twenty?"

"Couple of things jumped out at me from the articles. First, Randolph claimed to have an alibi. An alibi corroborated by several others. Second, given his alibi, his subsequent confession surprised the police. It seems like he could have gotten away with murder had he just kept quiet. The investigation wasn't pointing toward him, no evidence was stacked against him. Yet, he confessed as the police attempted to search for the killer."

"Guilty conscience, perhaps?"

I pointed at him as I sipped my beer. "Same thing I suspected. He lies to the police, but the guilt weighs on him. After so long, he can't take it any more and confesses."

"But?" Pap prompted, realizing I didn't subscribe fully to that theory.

"But… several other people confirmed his alibi."

"Lying for the Lord?" Pap suggested.

"My suspicions exactly. But again… every one of these servants was so loyal they didn't crack?"

"Perhaps the police didn't pressure them. Perhaps he chose his most loyal servants to lie for him."

"All valid points. But this house of cards collapses if even one of them who would have worked with Andrew daily feels the slightest pang of guilt. And again, if he has the wherewithal to plan such an elaborate cover to get away with murder, would he lack the ability to follow through and get away with murder?"

"Guilt plays all sorts of games. But I can understand the explanation leaves something to be desired."

"So, I agreed to check it out with Cate, as you know. Because you wouldn't help me talk her out of it."

"She's your MacKenzie to deal with, Jackie," he said with a chuckle. "So, you've been investigating and what are your thoughts now?"

"After meeting Randolph and interacting with him on several occasions now, I'm less certain he's guilty, to be honest."

Pap cocked his head at me, signaling me to continue.

"He's a nice guy! Friendly, well-mannered, seems happy in his marriage, has a new son and heir."

"Part of you still expects he may be guilty, though, right?"

"Yes," I admitted. "Less than eighty percent at this point. I'd put it more around sixty, maybe fifty. But yes, a large part of me thinks he may be guilty.

"He's a nice guy, this lowers your expectation he can commit murder. Got that part. Now, what makes you assume he's guilty?

"A few things. This Andrew character is a real bastard. I can imagine more than a few people would prefer him gone. It's not a stretch that he's murdered. Hell, even I don't like the guy."

Pap raised his eyebrows at that last statement. I explained before I went any further. "He's been a bit threatening toward Cate."

"Ah, that'll do it," Pap answered. "Continue."

"Earlier today, Cate and I traveled back. We witnessed an altercation between Andrew and Randolph. It was heated.

We couldn't hear what they said, but it was clear Randolph wasn't happy. He got rough with Andrew. So, it's not out of the question that the violence escalated into murder.

"Any hint of motive?"

"The woman in the tower room would be my best guess. Cate and I confirmed her existence there on a previous trip. There's some issue between Randolph and Andrew that resulted in an argument. And we know Andrew is aware of the woman in the tower. Cate found him in the tower room earlier today. Both Andrew and Randolph have lied to us about what's in that room. And Andrew threatened Cate as a result of her finding him near the tower.

"It's plausible that he killed Andrew over this secret," Pap agreed. "So, why is forty percent of you still questioning his guilt?"

"Gut feeling says he's not. Perhaps I'm being buffaloed, perhaps he's a fantastic liar. But my gut says he's innocent."

"Anything else?

"And Cate insists he's innocent.

"He's her great-great-great-grandfather. No one wants to face the possibility their ancestor was a violent killer."

"Yeah, I realize her vision is clouded by her familial ties but... I don't know, maybe it's a foolish hope, but I trust her judgment."

"That's good. You need to trust each other's judgment."

I nodded in agreement.

"What's next?" Pap asked.

"We're returning tomorrow to investigate. I pray Cate's right and we find evidence to prove his innocence but... at the end of the day, there's a very real possibility that Randolph MacKenzie is a murderer."

CHAPTER 20

October 29
8:17 p.m.

*P*ap and I finished the beers, turning our discussion to a lighter topic before I returned home. The beverage along with the added hours to my day eased me straight to sleep, so I didn't dwell on the mystery all night after finishing yesterday's journal entry. We returned to the past again today to search for clues.

I met Cate in the library following breakfast.

"Good morning!" Cate exclaimed. Her smile beamed across the room, her blue eyes sparkling with enthusiasm for the trip ahead. Also excited were Riley and Bailey. Riley bounded toward me to shower me with kisses. Bailey, still a bit shy, approached cautiously.

"Good morning, Lady Cate," I said as I stooped to pet the pups.

"With all the commotion yesterday, I forgot to ask if you spotted that murder weapon anywhere."

119

"No, I didn't. Though I only took a few cursory glances through most of the downstairs rooms after we split up."

"Cursory glance? I expected a thorough search," Cate teased.

"I found myself distracted by a certain someone disappearing up the stairs to chase after Andrew."

"I'll admit that could have gone better," Cate answered. "Anyway, I was only teasing."

"So, we need to search for the murder weapon today," I suggested.

"Yes," Cate agreed.

"We should keep out of sight. I'd prefer not to try skulking around the castle in search of a murder weapon while people know we're there."

"That's probably the best idea. We can't really explain why we'd like to go on another tour of the castle."

"Speaking of, I don't recall spotting that paperweight on our last tour."

"Me either, though I'll admit I wasn't exactly searching for a bronze globe paperweight."

"True. With the number of knick-knacks filling this place, it's not likely it'd stick out to us."

"Okay, so we search for the paperweight while avoiding everyone in the castle. It's probably best to split up..."

"Whoa!" I exclaimed. "Hold it right there."

"What?" Cate inquired.

"No splitting up, Cate. You're not supposed to be traipsing about the castle after what happened yesterday."

"But we're avoiding everyone! It should be fine. Besides, it's faster this way. The longer we're there, the better the chances are we get caught."

I shook my head at her. "Cate..." I began.

"Just... think about it," Cate interrupted.

"Fine, I'll consider it. Meet in two hours? Usual spot?"

"Yep!" Cate answered.

After a few morning chores, I headed into the castle to change. Cate met me on the dot of the hour, ready to go. We arrived in the closet in 1856. The bedroom beyond was empty. We crept to the door and inched it open. No one was in the hall beyond.

"Okay, you take the downstairs, I'll take up here," Cate whispered as she turned the doorknob to exit.

"No, Cate!" I hissed back. "No splitting up!"

"You agreed!"

"I agreed to think about it, not to do it!"

"It's faster this way!"

"But it's not safer," I contended.

"We're avoiding everyone, it should be fine!"

"We're TRYING to avoid everyone, that doesn't mean we'll succeed."

"We're less conspicuous alone than together!" Cate insisted.

"Ugh!" I groaned.

"We're wasting time! The longer we spend here, the more likely we are to get caught."

"Fine, fine. You win. You take upstairs, I'll take downstairs."

Cate nodded and spun toward the door. "Cate!" I breathed as I grabbed her arm. "Be careful. No risky stunts!"

Cate gave me a tight-lipped nod before she swung the door open and disappeared down the hall. I watched her as she scurried away from me. That lassie was too spirited for her own good. I needed to complete my search, though. I turned away from Cate's disappearing form and hurried to a back staircase. I glanced down its length before I raced downstairs.

I poked my head into a few rooms. I did not spot the paperweight, though. To be fair, I wasn't giving it my all.

Worry clouded my focus and pervaded my every thought. A bad feeling settled in my gut. Why had Cate insisted on splitting up? The lassie had a plan. One she didn't want me to be a part of.

I stood in a rarely used parlor, contemplating my options. The paperweight wasn't in the main sitting room, of that I was certain. It likely wasn't in the tea room, Cate would have noticed it, I surmised. I dare not try Randolph's office, though I doubted it was there. I would have noticed it in my time there.

On a whim, I abandoned my search and navigated to the nearest staircase. I climbed the steps two at a time, intent on locating Cate. My heart pounded as I hurried through the halls, my head on a swivel.

If my intuition proved correct, I doubted I'd find her except in one place: the tower room. I hastened through the halls toward it. I quickened my pace as I overheard a loud voice.

As I rounded the corner, I spotted Andrew, his hand gripping Cate's arm as he dragged her away from the turret stairs. Fury fueled my final steps toward them. How dare he manhandle Cate like that!

"Excuse me!" I shouted as I marched toward them. "Unhand my wife, sir!"

"Your wife, sir," he spat, dropping Cate's arm, "has been skulking around the castle. Again. I caught her at the tower door."

"I would hardly call it skulking. My cousin, Lord MacKenzie, has given us free access to the property, including the castle. You have no business telling either of us where we are or are not permitted."

"Yes," Cate chimed in. "What are you hiding up there?"

Andrew narrowed his eyes and scowled, offering an annoyed stare. "I am merely stating that you, madam," he said, turning his glare to Cate, "should take care when roaming the estate. You may find yourself in harm's way."

"I don't appreciate the veiled threat," I retorted.

"No threat at all, sir, just friendly advice. Now if you will excuse me, I have several duties to attend to." Andrew turned on his heel and ascended the tower stairs.

"Thanks," Cate whispered, raising her eyes to meet mine.

"Let's go," I said. The experience still upsets me, but I couldn't pinpoint if Andrew frustrated me or Cate's behavior.

Cate didn't argue, instead, she plodded down the hall in front of me and straight back to the closet. We used the time-piece to return to our time. As the second hand ticked at normal speed, I spoke again. "Are you mad?" I shouted, louder than I intended.

"I'm sorry!" Cate said with a sigh. "I found nothing in the bedrooms. We need more information! Information that's only in the tower room. They're hiding someone there, or something important!" Cate stalked into the bedroom and paced the floor.

I followed her. "Are you kidding me, Cate? Do you hear yourself? That man has threatened you twice now! He caught you somewhere you shouldn't have been, manhandled you down the stairs and who knows what he would have done next if I hadn't shown up! And all you can think about is what's he hiding?"

"Yes, all those things you mentioned means it must be something big! And what were you doing there? You must have had the same idea I did!"

"I doubt that. I finished my search downstairs and didn't see you anywhere else upstairs. I suspected where you were. I hoped I was wrong, but I wasn't."

"We need to go back tomorrow. Try to find something, anything! We're two days away from the murder!"

I sighed and shook my head, collecting my thoughts before I answered. "Cate, I really think we need to rethink this."

"We can't. We need to follow through. No tower runs this time, I promise. Let's go back and observe. We're so close to the murder, there's got to be some telltale signs! We have to use everything we know to get information!"

The stubborn lassie frustrated me to no end. But I, too, wanted to finish what we started. Though not at the expense of any harm coming to either of us. "Okay," I yielded. "But no more stunts. I'm serious, Cate!"

Cate held her hands up, signaling surrender. "I have that meeting with Mrs. Campbell tomorrow about the next party. We can go after lunch, mid-afternoon?"

"It's a plan," I acquiesced.

With that, we parted ways. I worked to put the entire incident out of my mind as I finished my day. This pursuit was becoming dangerous. Though Cate would never forgive me if we missed the Halloween ball. So, we at least had to make one more trip. And, as Cate argued, it was best going into that one with as much information as possible.

As it stands, though, today gave us no more information, only a better understanding of why someone may want Andrew dead. I've now got my odds at sixty-forty on Randolph's guilt.

CHAPTER 21

October 30
7:34 p.m.

Another reconnaissance mission to the past today. Not before a meeting between Lady Cate and the party czar, Mrs. Campbell. The persistent woman is now onto not one but two winter holiday parties: one for Christmas and one for New Year's Eve. Heaven help us. And on top of that, she's requesting we bring in a snow machine in the event the weather fails to cooperate. She's mad. This is more shocking than time traveling, to be honest!

After lunch, Cate and I headed back to 1856. We had no plan, totally winging it, which made me nervous. I said as much as I knocked on the front door.

Cate agreed. "I'm not sure what else we can do except observe and gather more information," she added. "We're so close to the murder, something, anything, may be a clue or tip us off. We need to keep our eyes and ears open."

"I like that. Observe only, good idea," I said as Thomson opened the door.

"Ah, Mr. and Mrs. MacKenzie, please come in. I shall announce your arrival." We entered the foyer.

"We're not expected. I hope it's not an inconvenience," I informed him.

"I'm sure it won't be. You're family, sir. You may wait in the sitting room."

We proceeded to the room off the foyer and Randolph joined us after a few moments.

"Jack, Catherine, lovely to see you," Randolph greeted us.

"My apologies, we come unannounced. My wife has borrowed one of your books and wanted to return it as soon as she had finished."

"Think nothing of it, you're family! Family is always welcome!" Randolph poured a drink for me and one for himself. Victoria entered, rushing to Cate to embrace her. "You've missed little, my dear, just our cousins apologizing for disturbing our peace."

"You are never disturbing us," Victoria assured us.

"We apologize for coming unannounced. But I have finished with the book I borrowed and wanted to return it."

"You needn't make a special trip, but I will not object as I do love to see you," Victoria said as she rang the wall bell to call the servants.

"Truth be told," Cate said, "I hoped to return it and select another."

"By all means! I must make time to read, as you do, Catherine," Victoria said as Thompson entered. Victoria requested tea for herself and Cate.

We discussed plans for the ball tomorrow evening, agreeing to arrive early to dress at the castle. When the ladies finished their tea, Victoria ushered Cate upstairs to show her the necklace she planned to wear to the ball.

Left alone with Randolph, I excused him from any obligation to play host. "Well, I shan't keep you any longer, cousin.

I am capable to wait for my wife's return on my own. I'm sure you have business to attend to."

Randolph pulled the timepiece from his pocket and glanced at it. "Yes, if you do not mind waiting alone, I do have something pressing that requires my attention."

"Not at all, cousin."

"I dare say, though, you may be in for a long wait. I fear ladies discussing clothing and jewelry may take longer than discussions in the House of Lords!" Randolph roared with laughter at his own joke as he disappeared through the door.

He may be correct, I reflected. Even if he was, it provided me the opportunity for one more peek around. I'd done a shoddy job yesterday and so far, we'd found nothing that hinted at the upcoming tragedy.

I waited for a few moments for Randolph to disappear before I began my search of the downstairs. I popped in and out of several rooms, this time checking each with a discerning eye. I continued down the hall toward the library. My eyes scanned the room as I entered. Just inside the door, a scrap of paper lay on the floor. I snatched it from the hardwood and glanced at it for a moment before continuing my search.

I did a double-take as I recognized the addressee. My eyes widened as I read the words scrawled on the grainy paper in black ink.

Catherine–I must see you, it's urgent. Meet me at the loch at 3:30.

-Randolph

Oh, no. My stomach dropped and my mouth went dry. Randolph wasn't meeting Cate. This was a ruse. One Cate was most likely unaware of. Whatever purpose was behind it could not be honorable. I cursed allowing her out of my sight as I rushed from the library to the nearest door. I sprinted down the path to the loch.

As I approached, I overheard the sound of an argument. "Let go!" Cate screamed.

My heart pounded in my chest as I raced toward the water. I crested the hill with the loch lying below me. Andrew held Cate by the arms. She struggled against him, but he backed her into the loch. With one final shove, Cate toppled backward, tumbling into the icy waters.

She flailed as she struggled to stay afloat, but the heavy fabric she wore proved too much for her. I raced headlong toward the water's edge as Cate slipped below the surface.

I dove into the loch the moment my feet hit the bank's edge. My hands searched the icy waters for Cate. I saw her porcelain hand reaching toward the surface and surged toward it. I grasped it and tugged. With my other hand, I grasped her body, wrapping my arm around her waist. I hauled her upward and dragged her onto the bank. She choked and coughed. I laid her on her side as I knelt over her. "Cate! Cate! Are you all right?"

Cate gulped for air but nodded. "Yes," she choked out. "I'm okay." After another moment, she pulled herself to sitting. I collapsed back onto the bank next to her, breathing a sigh of relief.

"Thank you," Cate murmured. "Lucky you found me when you did."

"Aye, damn lucky. If I wasn't so relieved you're alive, I would let you have it for sneaking off like that. No splitting up, remember?"

"Yes, I remember. But I got a note from Randolph. Well, that's what it said, anyway. It told me to meet him at the loch and I had no time to find you."

"I know. I found the note on the library floor when I was poking around. I came as quickly as I could. Not fast enough to stop that bastard from tossing you into the loch, but at least fast enough to stop him from killing you. Cate, you've got to be more careful!"

"I know, I know," Cate conceded. "I'm sorry. I wasn't thinking." Cate grasped the folds of her dress and wrung water from it. "I suppose we should get back. I'd like to get home and change into something warm and dry."

"Me, too. Assuming we still can, that is."

"Why wouldn't..." Cate began as my comment sunk in. She'd just nearly sunk to the bottom of the loch. Around her neck hung a centuries-old timepiece. Had the water seeped inside and damaged it, I wondered?

"THE WATCH!" Cate exclaimed.

"Aye, the watch."

Cate grasped at the chain around her neck and tugged the watch from under her dress. She snapped open the cover. The second-hand ticked ever-so-slowly. "It's still working, hopefully it's not damaged."

"Let's not wait to find out. Let's go." I pulled myself to standing and offered Cate a hand. "Let's go before it breaks."

"Okay," she agreed, grasping my hand. We hurried to the castle and said a silent prayer as we rubbed the timepiece. It sped up, and we both breathed a sigh of relief. "Oh, I hope that worked and we're home," Cate said.

"Only one way to find out," I offered.

Cate exited the closet and raced into the hall and toward her bedroom suite. She burst through the doors, calling for the pups. Both dogs raced toward her. "We're back!" Cate cried.

"Thank heavens," I said.

"At least we haven't broken the watch."

"It may be better if we had."

"No! We still have the murder to solve and Randolph's reputation to save!" Cate countered.

"Yes, I realize that. But I'm less happy about it now than I was before. This is becoming dangerous, and we've taken a reckless chance that may have stranded us in the 1800s!"

"It's more dangerous because we're on to something!" Cate said. "What or who is in that tower room that has Andrew so apprehensive that he's willing to kill for it?"

"I can't believe you're still so interested even after what happened," I said with a shake of my head. "Oh, Lady Cate, I'll never figure you out."

Cate's face fell, and she drew her mouth into a thin line. "To be honest, I'm still shaken by it. I guess it's how I deal with anything unpleasant, throw myself into the 'research' I'm working on."

"That, my dear Lady Cate, is called avoidance." I grinned at her. Okay, the poor lassie realized the mistake she'd made. I didn't want to make her feel worse than she already did. "I'm going to get out of these wet clothes. You should do the same." I backed toward the door and gave a grand bow before disappearing through it. "M'lady."

"Oh, Jack," Cate said, stopping me.

"Yeah?"

"Thanks again. You're a lifesaver."

I groaned. "Oh, that's a terrible joke, Lady Cate, just terrible."

She grinned and stuck her tongue out at me before I disappeared down the hall.

As I stripped off my soaked clothes, the incident ran through my mind again. We were damn lucky Cate didn't meet her end before she was born! One day away from the murder. This guy couldn't die soon enough for me. At this point, I'd like to learn who did it so I can award them a medal.

CHAPTER 22

October 31
5:50 a.m.

Today's the big day. My stomach is tied in knots. The next time I write, a murder will have taken place. A murder I realize ahead of time will happen and am doing nothing to stop. As much as I insisted to Cate we couldn't, that idea suddenly makes me feel like a real heel. Still, saving Andrew's life may leave too many ripples in time. We must stay the course.

I'll be distracted all day until this event happens. As well-prepared as we are (realizing there will be a murder, who the victim is, how it happened), I feel totally and wholly unprepared for this.

The real tragedy here is that I have to change into old-fashioned clothing not once but twice! I shouldn't joke. A man is about to lose his life. Though, I still believe my predicament comes in a close second.

* * *

9:03 p.m.

Andrew is dead. The crime occurred just as we suspected. Despite being prepared, it was really unbelievable to live through it. I'll start at the beginning.

Cate and I returned to 1856 and took our usual circuit out of the castle and around to the front door. Within minutes, we were ushered inside, and Cate was swept off to dress with Victoria.

Thompson gathered my formalwear, carried in a garment bag and informed me he would place it in a private bedroom for me to dress in later. He suggested I join Randolph in the sitting room. The castle was abuzz with activity. Servants rushed about, adding final touches and preparing for the onslaught of guests.

I entered the room off the foyer and found Randolph nursing a scotch in an armchair.

"Jack!" he exclaimed. His face brightened, and a smile formed on his lips. He leapt from his seat and poured a glass of scotch, then refilled his glass. "Scotch? I won't take no for an answer." He handed the glass to me.

"Don't mind if I do," I said, accepting the drink.

"Sit down," he said and motioned to a chair.

I sunk into it, feeling the heat of the nearby fireplace. If it were up to me, I'd have stayed by the fire for the entire evening, though Cate would be highly disappointed in me if I chose that.

"Quite a commotion out there," I noted as I stared into the amber liquid.

Randolph issued a grunt. "Yes, yes. It will be quite a night."

"Indeed," I answered. An ironic choice of words, I mused.

"If it were all the same to me, I'd forego the pomp and

circumstance and have several good friends over for a few drinks and some laughs."

I chuckled at Randolph's statement. "I'd concur with that sentiment," I answered.

"Catherine dragged you by the lapels, eh?" he teased.

"Something like that," I answered.

"Well, Victoria is thrilled you both are attending, so I appreciate your efforts despite the disruption to your evening."

I sipped the scotch and nodded at him. "These evenings are important to Victoria," Randolph explained further. "Therefore, they are important to me. And I cannot say I do not enjoy them. It is great fun to witness the merrymaking."

"I'm not much of a merrymaker, sir," I admitted.

"Just like a Reid," Randolph answered with a grin.

Randolph pulled the timepiece from his vest pocket. With a sigh, he announced, "I suppose we should dress." He swallowed the rest of his Scotch and set the glass on the table. I followed suit. "I'll show you to where you can change. I arranged for a valet to assist you."

Before I could object, Randolph opened the door to an upstairs bedroom where Thomson awaited us. "Ah, Thomson," Randolph said. "Did you arrange a valet for Mr. MacKenzie?"

"I shall see to him myself, m'lord."

"Excellent, excellent. You're in good hands with Thomson. I shall see you soon, Jack." Randolph clapped me on the back before departing from the room.

I nodded to him as he stepped out before returning my gaze to Thomson. Valet, my mind questioned, was he serious? I offered an awkward smile to the man as I stepped further into the room. I spotted my evening wear ready on a wooden clothes rack. "I'm certain you have many things to attend to, Thomson. I am sure I can manage on my own."

"I wouldn't hear of it, sir!" Thomson insisted. "I shall be most happy to assist you."

I swallowed hard. This guy wasn't taking no for an answer, I realized. Best to get the awkward experience over with, I figured. I unbuttoned my coat and began to remove it. "Allow me, sir," Thomson said. He circled around me and pulled the jacket off, carefully creasing it and laying it across the bed to be dealt with later.

I cleared my throat as I continued removing my garments. Thomson darted around the room, attending to any discarded garments and supplying their replacements. He fastened my cufflinks before assisting me in sliding on my jacket. As I buttoned its front, Thomson brushed off any lint.

"Thank you, Thomson," I responded after I'd finished dressing.

"You are quite welcome, sir. Is there anything else?"

"No, that is all, thank you."

"Very good, sir. Lord MacKenzie left instructions that he will meet you here before you proceed downstairs."

"Fine," I said with a nod. My collar had already begun to irritate me.

"I shall take my leave, Mr. MacKenzie," Thomson said with a small bow.

Left to my own devices, I wandered to the window and glanced over the autumn landscape. The deep red sun hung low in the October sky. Streaks of red and purple painted the horizon. As the sun lowered, I couldn't help but be reminded that for one of us within the castle's walls, this was the last sunset he'd experience.

A knock at the door interrupted my thoughts. "Come in!" I called.

"Ready?" Randolph asked as he pushed through the door.

"Yes," I replied.

"We have time for one more drink," Randolph noted. He poured two small glasses of Scotch from a drink cart and handed one to me. He raised his glass to me before he imbibed. "To you and Catherine. We are most fortunate to have met and known you."

I smiled at the sentiment. If Randolph was the murderer, no one would have guessed it at this moment. We finished our drinks.

"Shall we retrieve the ladies?" Randolph inquired.

I agreed and followed Randolph to another bedroom. He knocked at the door and asked if we could enter. "Just a moment!" Victoria's voice called. After a moment, she followed up with, "We are ready!"

Randolph pushed the door open, and I followed him into the room. Victoria and Cate stood inside in contrasting dresses. Victoria's assessment proved correct. Cate looked radiant in her blue gown. Her blue eyes seemed bluer than normal, and her porcelain skin radiated.

"Well, if these aren't two angels descended straight from heaven in front of us, cousin," Randolph said as he took Victoria's hands and admired her before kissing her cheek. "You look lovely, my dear. Simply lovely."

"Thank you, husband. How kind. And how handsome you are!" Victoria answered.

This guy was a hard act to follow, but I did my best. I approached Cate. "So, this is the infamous dress. It has lived up to its potential. You look beautiful, Catherine." I leaned forward and kissed her cheek, hoping it didn't appear as awkward as it felt.

"Thank you. I must thank Victoria for the necklace. It is a perfect match!"

"Oh, it pales when compared to your beauty, cousin Catherine!" Randolph said. He checked the timepiece. "We should proceed downstairs. Guests will arrive soon! Shall we?" He offered Victoria his arm, which she accepted. I did the same with Cate, and we followed our hosts to the ballroom.

As we entered the mammoth room, Cate and Victoria chatted about the ambiance. I spotted an orchestra and swallowed hard. With no knowledge of any form of dance from this era, I realized how ill-prepared I was to be at a ball.

As we took our places to await the first guests, Andrew arrived in the ballroom, delivering items from the kitchen. He glared at Cate after doing a double-take.

"Your friend looks happy to see you," I whispered.

"Yes, he seems downright tickled," she answered.

"Don't go sneaking off anywhere out of my sight," I warned.

"Don't worry, I won't," Cate agreed.

"Good, it'd be a terrible shame to ruin that dress."

Cate gave my chest a light smack over the poor joke. "It is interesting to see the similarities between our ball and theirs," Cate commented as guests filtered in.

"Lucky for us, the biggest difference was no one was killed at ours."

Any further conversation was cut off as Randolph and Victoria called us over to meet several guests. After most guests arrived, Victoria ushered Cate around the room while Randolph escorted me, introducing me to various people.

My mind numbed as names, ranks and lineage of guest after guest was thrown at me. Finally, we collected refreshments for Cate and Victoria and approached them. I handed a glass off to Cate. She accepted it, staring at the glass I held in my hand. Cate raised her eyebrows at it, then stared at me.

What was wrong with her, I wondered? She gave me another hard gaze, then flitted her eyes to the glass. After her third try, I understood. I downed my drink and announced I needed another. After asking if anyone else needed a refill, Cate and I excused ourselves.

"I didn't think you'd ever pick up on that," Cate said as we walked away.

"Your skills at charades are weak, Lady Cate."

I retrieved another drink, and we found a corner to speak privately. "Anything interesting on your end?" Cate asked.

"Nothing of note. I've heard enough about land deals, the House of Lords, and almost everyone asked me if my wife knew anything about the impending conflict in the States. But no hints why someone will soon be murdered."

"Randolph was never away from you, right?"

"Never. What about on your end?"

"I heard less than you! All my talk was about marriages, births, parties and clothing. Oh, and one discussion about the best painter for a handsome portrait."

"Do you think Victoria may have killed him? And Randolph covered for her? He seems protective of her."

"But why?" Cate questioned. "It doesn't fit her personality at all, and she doesn't seem to have much to hide. In fact, she seems an open book in the discussions I've had with her."

"I just can't figure out who else he'd be covering for if he didn't do it."

"I don't know. It must deal with that mysterious woman in the tower. Now would be a perfect time to meet her, but we can't leave the party."

"And we will NOT split up," I insisted.

"No, you're right. I don't want to end up thrown down the tower stairs by Andrew. I'd end up dead before I was born!"

Any further conversation was stopped by Randolph tapping his glass in the middle of the room. Quietness fell over the crowd and Randolph welcomed everyone. After the applause died down, Randolph praised Victoria's efforts to pull together the grand event. His words chilled me. "This ball will be remembered for years," he said, with little idea how true that would be.

After his speech, he led Victoria to the middle of the floor to begin the dancing. Cate and I inched toward the wall. Discomfort washed over me as I prayed I wouldn't have to attempt a waltz.

As if reading my mind, Cate said, "I'm hoping to avoid any dancing. I imagine it would be a dead giveaway that we're not from this century."

"No kidding," I responded. "I've got no idea what they're doing."

"At least we can easily account for Randolph's whereabouts!"

We survived through several dances before Randolph and Victoria approached us.

"Wallflowers, are we?" Randolph inquired.

"I'm sorry to say we are," I responded.

"Oh, surely, cousin Jack, you'll dance with your lovely wife!" Victoria said.

"I think she'd prefer I didn't. I've two left feet, and her toes would never survive it!"

Cate nodded to provide me backup. "I'm happy to watch the fun," she said.

"Nonsense, cousin Catherine!" Randolph exclaimed. "I shall have the next dance and I shall not step on your toes!"

"Oh, really, that's not..." Cate tried.

Randolph waved her comment away before she finished it. "Now, I won't take no for an answer," Randolph insisted. He grabbed Cate's hand and pulled her toward the dance floor.

"Do not worry, cousin Catherine, I shall keep Jack company while I rest for the next round!" Victoria laughed and waved them on.

Cate offered me a wide-eyed and panicked glance as Randolph led her away. I offered an encouraging yet uncertain half-smile to her. Poor Cate, I mused. I was lucky Victoria didn't strong-arm me into a dance.

Randolph led Cate to the center of the floor. They spoke a few words before Randolph grabbed hold of Cate. With a grin on his face, he swung her around the dance floor. After a few moments, a smile spread across her face. It was contagious, and I found myself grinning at her waltz. No experience with a waltz, Lady Cate, I thought? The lassie's skills were indistinguishable from the other dancers.

As the dance ended, Andrew approached Randolph. Just as Andrew leaned toward Randolph, an older gentleman approached Victoria and requested a dance. She agreed, excusing herself from my company. As she departed, I returned my gaze to the room's center. Randolph was gone. Cate hurried across the dance floor. With wide eyes, she signaled for me to follow her with a slight tilt of her head.

"What's up?" I asked as I rejoined Cate, who headed for the doorway.

"Andrew just said something to Randolph. He seemed agitated and excused himself to attend to 'urgent business.' Something's up, we need to follow him."

"Did you see where he went?" I inquired.

"Yes, down this hall. There!" A beam of light streamed into the hallway from an open door.

I held my fingers to my lips to signal silence. We crept toward the door. Loud voices carried into the hall.

"… will NOT continue to be threatened in my own home!" Randolph shouted.

"Don't look like you've got much choice the way I see it," Andrew retorted. Cate shot me a glance.

"Do not presume to tell me what I have and haven't," Randolph blasted him.

"What you HAVE is a secret whore," Andrew snarled.

"How dare you, sir?" Randolph retorted.

"How dare I? How dare I? How dare YOU! Asking me to wait on your whore, fetching this and that, all the while asking me to keep quiet about it. And nothing in it for me."

A scuffle sounded from within. Through the crack in the door, I spotted Randolph lunge toward Andrew and grasp him by the collar.

"Now you listen to me, you sorry excuse for a man, this ends tonight! I shall pay you what you ask, and you shall vacate this property and never return."

Andrew shook Randolph's hands from his neck. "You'd turn me out on the street given the information I have on you? That wouldn't be wise."

Randolph smirked. "Any tale you tell now will be the sour grapes of a released staff member. No one will believe you. Now collect your things and go. AFTER you've attended to Sonia."

"You're making a huge mistake, friend. You've no idea the lengths I'll go to to protect what's mine. Just ask Catherine MacKenzie."

Andrew spun on his heel and exited the room. Cate and I shrunk into the shadows, flattening ourselves against the wall. In his rage, Andrew stormed past our hiding spot, unaware of our presence. We followed his retreating figure with our eyes.

When we turned back, Randolph stood in the doorway. "Catherine… Jack…" he stumbled. "I… I must apologize for my prolonged absence. I hope I haven't been missed."

"Randolph…" I began, not certain where I was going with the statement.

Cate shoved Randolph inside the room. "Randolph, we must speak with you. We overheard your conversation with Andrew. He must leave the house now!"

"Catherine!" Randolph exclaimed. "What is the meaning of this?"

"Perhaps you should be the one explaining that. What is the problem with Andrew? We saw you the other day at the loch and overheard you tonight. What is he threatening you with? Who is Sonia?"

My mind swirled as Cate rapid-fired questions at Randolph. In a panic, Cate attempted to save both Randolph and Andrew by insisting Andrew leave the property before his death.

"I can't answer those questions, Catherine. I'm sorry," Randolph responded.

"Damn it, Randolph, now isn't the time to be tight-lipped!" Cate shouted.

Randolph wore an expression of surprise at Cate's overzealous statement. "She's only trying to help," I chimed in. "We need the answers to those questions." While I preferred not to alter history, Malcolm's words rung in my head: protect, Jack, protect.

"Why?" Randolph inquired. "What do you know?"

Cate glanced at me. Her forehead wrinkled, and she wore a dismayed expression. "Nothing we can share," I said.

"I'm afraid I am the same. With nothing to share. But perhaps you can answer this. Why did my footman suggest I ask you about the lengths he's willing to go to in order to protect what is his?"

Cate sighed. "We can't…" I began.

Cate interrupted me. "He pushed me into the loch yesterday after catching me wandering in the castle a few times. I almost drowned. I was lucky Jack pulled me out before anything happened to me."

"My God, Catherine! Are you quite all right? You should have informed me at once!"

"It's difficult to explain. I don't… this time traveling is so difficult to navigate. You must accept there are things we can't share with you."

Randolph paused for a moment before responding. "I understand. But I ask you to offer me the same consideration." Silence fell between us. None of us willing to give in to the other's point of view.

Randolph spoke again after a moment. "I relieved him of his position. He'll soon be gone from this house, so he shan't be bothering you again. Now, we should return to the party before we are missed."

Cate nodded, though I sensed her reluctance. A clock in the room ticked the time away. Nearly time for the body to be discovered, I noted. Perhaps our presence altered things in some way, and we'd avoid the entire murder.

"You go ahead without me, I need a moment. I shall be right behind you," Randolph said.

Cate glanced at me. "Go! I will be fine!" Randolph insisted.

Without a word, we filed from the room. "Do you think we should have left him?" I inquired.

"I'm not sure we had a choice," Cate admitted. "It's almost time for the murder anyway. Maybe we somehow avoided it."

As we entered the ballroom, Victoria sought us out. "There you are! Have you seen Randolph? He seems to have disappeared!"

Cate smiled at her. "Oh, he was right behind us. We were discussing a painting and stepped out to view it. I'm afraid it was our fault. He should be here any moment."

"A painting?" Victoria questioned. "He left my ball for a painting?"

"Yes," I confirmed, following up on Cate's fib. "A family portrait. My sincere apologies, Victoria. I'm afraid I was somewhat overzealous in asking about an ancestor. Randolph is a gracious host."

"Yes," Cate added. "Again, we're so very sorry for stealing him away."

"No apology needed, dear cousins. I was hoping to have another dance with him though."

"I'm sure he will be here any moment," Cate said.

Within a few minutes, Victoria's face brightened, and she waved across the room. "Ah, there he is!"

Randolph approached and kissed Victoria's cheek.

"Viewing a painting while we have a ball ongoing? Honestly, Randolph! You are a terrible host!" Victoria teased, a grin on her face.

"Well…" Randolph began when a blood-curdling scream tore through the ballroom. The band ceased playing and the dancers ground to a halt. Hushed silence fell over the entire room.

One of the servants raced into the room. "M'lord, you'd better come quick."

"What is it?" Victoria asked as the smile faded from her face. Cate and I shared a glance, knowing all too well what it was.

"Stay with Victoria," I suggested as I followed Randolph through the door.

We stepped into the cool night air. A few guests milled around outside. A group fussed over a woman who swooned. I glanced from her to the scene in front of me. Several men stood in a circle. As they stepped back, I caught sight of what they surrounded. Andrew Forsythe's dead body lay sprawled on the ground.

CHAPTER 23

October 31
10:23 p.m.

The gruesome sight burned itself into my memory.

"Andrew!" Randolph exclaimed at the sight. "My God!"

"Careful not to disturb the scene," I cautioned everyone. "Someone must summon the police."

"They've been sent for," a gentleman responded.

"Yes, yes," Randolph agreed. "Good." He murmured, sounding unsure, unlike himself.

I stared at him as he took stock of the gruesome display. He appeared shocked. Was he, I wondered? Did he not see this coming? Or was he a fantastic actor?

As I pondered Randolph's guilt, he spoke. "My God, Catherine! You shouldn't be here!"

I spun and spotted Cate a few paces behind us. "Cate!" I called. "Er, Catherine!" I corrected as I raced toward her. "You don't want to see this, go inside." Cate nodded without speaking. "We'll talk later."

I turned her away from the scene and sent her back to the ballroom. I returned to the crime scene. The blood pooled under Andrew's mangled body and spread into a large puddle. Randolph ran a shaky hand through his hair.

"We should return inside," I suggested. "Everyone will look to you for guidance. Are you able to put this aside as we deal with the situation?"

Randolph glanced at me, his brow furrowed and his mouth agape. After a moment, he said, "Yes, yes, I believe so. Lead the way, cousin Jack."

We rejoined Cate and Victoria in the ballroom. "Randolph?" Victoria inquired, her eyes searching his features for answers.

Randolph put his arms around her. "I'm sorry, my darling." He raised his voice. "And I am sorry to all our guests! There has been a tragedy tonight. Young Andrew, one of our footmen, has met with an accident that cost him his life." Gasps rang out in the room. "The police have been sent for. I ask that all of you please remain calm and within the ballroom until they have arrived. Thank you for your patience and please, despite the dreadful news, continue to enjoy the refreshments while you wait."

"How could this happen?" Victoria questioned.

"Come, darling, please sit down." Randolph guided her to a chair.

She sunk into it before springing up. "Oh, I should…" Victoria's voice trailed off as though she could not fathom anything suitable to do.

"Just rest, darling," Randolph soothed. "The police will be here any moment."

Cate and I remained several steps away from Randolph and Victoria. My concern turned from the couple to Cate. "Are you all right?"

"Yes, thank you. I'm fine. I wish I hadn't seen the body, but yes. Did you spot anything of interest?"

"Nothing more than we already know. The fall didn't kill him, as we read."

"It's that obvious?"

"Yes," I answered, recalling his smashed skull. "It was obvious."

"It couldn't..." Cate began when Randolph interrupted her.

He waved her toward him. "Catherine," he called. "Could you please stay with Victoria? She's taking the news rather poorly. I'm concerned. There are many things I should attend to, but I am reluctant to leave her."

"Certainly," Cate assured him. "Jack can help with anything you need."

"Thank you both. Jack, please follow me."

Randolph and I stepped away. We made our way toward the gardens outside, stopped several times by various guests. Randolph did his best to keep them calm and disclose little information. His handling was impressive, despite his shock immediately following the discovery.

Several officers arrived, and Randolph and I escorted them outside. Randolph explained the brief timeline as the officers studied the scene.

When we returned to the ballroom, officers were already requesting the guests to form lines and speak with a member of their department before leaving. I did not see Cate or Victoria. Within moments, though, Cate appeared in the doorway.

As the last of the guests filtered from the ballroom, Cate made her way to me. "We'd better get our stories straight," I breathed. "We only have a few moments."

"I plan to stick to the truth as much as I can," Cate answered. "We were with Randolph discussing a painting, then returned to the party. A few minutes passed before we heard the scream."

"What about Andrew?"

"Nothing. I don't plan on mentioning our run-ins with him. We'd have little reason to have engaged in many conversations with him. It shouldn't be a stretch."

"I agree. We say as little as possible."

Cate nodded as an officer approached us.

"Mr. and Mrs. MacKenzie, we'd like to speak with each of you. Perhaps Mrs. MacKenzie first so she may return to Lady MacKenzie and rest." Cate nodded. "If you'll follow me, Mrs. MacKenzie, you may have a seat here."

I waited as Cate spoke with the officer. After a few moments, she rose and led the man from the room. They must be going to speak with Victoria, I surmised.

He returned within ten minutes and approached me. "All right, Mr. MacKenzie, if you don't mind, could we speak now?"

"Of course," I obliged.

"And where were you when the discovery was made?" he began.

"Here, in the ballroom."

He nodded. "And you realized the problem how?"

"We heard a scream. One of the servants alerted Lord MacKenzie. He and I followed the servant outside and made the discovery."

"I see. And when had you last seen the deceased?"

"Uh, earlier this evening. He served at the party."

"Have you met the deceased prior to this evening?"

"Yes, of course. Well, not met, per se, rather, I have seen him in the castle whilst we visited."

"Of course, sir. Finally, have you any reason why the deceased may have taken his life?"

"No, though, as I mentioned, we were not acquainted. I

believe he served in the dining room during several of our visits. Beyond that, I have no personal knowledge of the deceased or his mindset."

The officer flipped his small notebook closed and nodded to me. "Thank you, Mr. MacKenzie. Awful business, this. We hope to have it cleaned up soon and be out of Lord MacKenzie's way."

"I'm certain he appreciates that. It is not the end to the evening we envisioned."

He nodded again as he left me to attend to other business. I rejoined Randolph. "I have relieved the staff of any obligations this evening. Given the shock, I think it best," he said.

"I'm certain they appreciate that."

"How terrible," Randolph said. "I can't help but feel somewhat responsible."

Responsible, my mind pinged. Was he admitting guilt? "I spoke so harshly to him. Dismissed him from his position. Did the news make him despondent enough to do this?"

Was Randolph innocent, my mind questioned again? Or was this a clever ploy to feign innocence?

"Randolph," I responded, "why did you dismiss Andrew? What were you two arguing about?"

"Hmm?" Randolph murmured. "Oh, I should check on Victoria."

Stonewalled again, I reflected as I followed him to Victoria's room. As we entered her sitting room, we found Bryson. She wrung her hands as she stared at the bedroom door. "Mrs. MacKenzie is with her, m'lord."

"Good," Randolph said with a nod.

"I shall check on them now." Bryson approached the door, giving it a light knock. She eased it open and poked her head inside. Within seconds, she backed from the door and Cate emerged.

"Victoria is asleep," Cate reported in a whisper.

"How is she?" Randolph inquired.

"Upset. Perhaps the sleep will do her good."

"You are calming for her, Catherine. Thank you." He took Cate's hands in his as he smiled at her.

"Randolph, we need to speak to you," Cate entreated.

A knocked sounded at the door. "Sir," a footman said as he peered in. "You're needed downstairs."

Randolph nodded and retreated to the door. Before pulling it shut behind him, he turned to us. "You two will return tomorrow, please?" he inquired. We nodded after exchanging a glance. "Good. Speak to you then. Excuse me."

"Well, I guess that's our cue," I said as Randolph disappeared.

"Yes, seems so," Cate agreed. "We should travel home. Just let me check on Victoria one more time." Cate eased the bedroom door open and peered in. Satisfied, she pulled it shut and reported, "She's asleep."

"Good, okay, let's go."

We navigated to the closet and returned to the present. Eight hours had passed in 1856. Only thirty minutes had passed in our time. Despite being exhausted, we both admitted we couldn't settle. We agreed to meet in the library after changing.

My mind raced as I slipped back into my normal clothing. The details of the evening replayed on a continual loop in my mind's eye.

I sauntered to the library; certain I had some time to kill. While beautiful, Cate's dress would take much longer to remove than my clothes. Exhaustion coursed through me as I entered the library. I collapsed in one of the generous armchairs. It felt like midnight to me, though it was mid-afternoon in our time.

I stood to greet Cate and crew as I heard the sound of galloping paws approaching from down the hall. Riley burst into the room and raced toward me. I grabbed him to say hello. His new pal, Bailey, approached slowly. The little fellow was still backward. I bent down to give his head a scratch.

"The new addition isn't as keen on me as Riley," I mentioned as Cate entered.

"I'm sure you'll win him over. Riley took an immediate shine to you, which is unusual for him. Bailey is more bashful than Riley. I'm sure he'll come around soon, though! He's had a tough start."

"Aye, but he's living the life of… well, Riley now!" I offered a hearty laugh at my ridiculous joke.

Cate groaned at me. "You should take your act on the road."

"I'll keep my day job, thanks. Or my night job, or whatever I've got here. I feel like I've lived through two days already and it's not even suppertime yet."

"Yes," Cate said, wincing as she eased into an armchair. "The only thing keeping me awake is fretting over Randolph and Victoria. I feel terrible for them both."

"Aye, so do I. I expected it and it was still a shock. I can imagine they are both reeling. Well, unless Randolph expected it, too."

"He couldn't have done it though, right?"

I considered it for a moment. Randolph's statement regarding feeling responsible flitted through my mind. "I don't know. Perhaps he could have. We weren't with him the entire time. There was a gap between when we returned to the party and when he returned."

"Yes, but was it a large enough gap for him to have committed a murder? I don't imagine so."

"It would have been a tight window but may be possible."

Cate paused for a moment, considering my statement. "Really tight," she answered. "It's safe to assume the body was thrown from the tower window based on where it landed, would you agree?"

"Yes, I'd consider that a reasonable assumption."

"Okay, so that means Randolph had to leave his office, locate Andrew, kill him with the globe paperweight by striking him with multiple blows, toss his body from the tower, discard the murder weapon in the tower room and return to the ballroom all within that small time frame. It doesn't seem possible."

"Well, assume Andrew was in the tower and Randolph knew it."

"Okay, that's a safe bet. And it would shave some time off, but still, that's a tall order to go to the tower, murder someone, throw his body out the window and make it back to the party within… what would you estimate it at? Perhaps five to seven minutes?"

"No longer than that, yes. And yes, that is a tall order."

"We could try it out and time it," Cate suggested.

"It's not a bad idea, although I was rather comfy here." Cate rolled her eyes at me. "Okay, okay, Lady Cate, we'll try it."

I dragged myself behind Cate as we headed to Randolph's office. "Okay," Cate instructed. "As soon as I leave, you go to the tower room, unlock it, pretend to bash someone multiple times with a paperweight, heave their body out the window then meet me in the ballroom."

"I never realized how teacher-like you really are, Lady Cate. Okay, got the timer ready on your phone?"

"Yes. Oh, give me a few moments' head start. We didn't see or hear Randolph leave his office when we were walking down the hall."

"Got it."

"Okay, here we go!" Cate started the timer and exited the room.

I stood in the doorway until she was far enough down the hall that I could slip from the office without alerting her. It took me fifty long and hurried steps to reach the corner. I broke into a full run as I rounded it. I raced through the hallways and to the upstairs and took the shortest route to the tower stairs.

The curving stairway rounded away from me to the tower room. I leapt up the stone steps two by two. I pretended to shove a key into the lock before I burst into the room. Using an imaginary paperweight that I guessed would be located near the door, I swung in the air three times. I tossed my fictitious paperweight to the side, lifted the invisible body and carried it to the window. I pushed the pane open, tossed the body out, closed the window and raced across the room.

With the door shut behind me, I scrambled down the stairs, ran the length of the castle to the stairs nearest the ballroom and descended them. I sprinted down the hall and entered the ballroom through the doors Randolph used.

"Time?" I gasped as I doubled over from the exertion. Sweat beaded on my forehead and I heaved in air.

"Seven minutes, forty-eight seconds."

"I had a few thoughts along the way," I choked.

"Let's go back to the library. Looks like you need a rest!"

"Great idea, Lady Cate!"

We made our way back to the library, and I sunk into an armchair. "So," Cate began, "that window is really tight. You were forty-eight seconds over the time frame we came up with. So, I'm not sure it helps." Cate frowned as she considered the lack of information the experiment provided.

"But as I spent a few moments thrashing my arms around pretending to murder someone with a brass paperweight, something occurred to me. This is a close contact crime. Is it likely he'd end up with no blood on him?"

"Oh! Great point! I didn't see any."

"Neither did I. And I doubt he had time to clean it off. I ran so we could determine the shortest amount of time Randolph would have had to commit the murder."

"By the sound and sight of you, it was much faster than Randolph would have. He wasn't out of breath and wasn't perspiring when he rejoined us."

"Maybe he's in better shape than me," I suggested. The glance Cate shot me bolstered my ego. "Thanks for the vote of confidence."

"Okay, we've ruled out Randolph as a suspect."

"I agree. The possibility is remote," I answered.

"One thing settled: Randolph is not the murderer. Two questions remain. Who is the real killer and why does Randolph cover for them?"

"Between the guests and the staff, there were over one hundred people. There's no way we could keep track of where everyone was. This is impossible, Cate."

"It's not. Would Randolph confess to a crime he didn't commit for the vast majority of the people there?"

"Good point," I conceded.

"That narrows the list. There are only two people I imagine he would protect."

I considered Cate's statement. "Victoria. She's the only one I can come up with."

"Victoria, yes. He'd do anything for her. But she's not the murderer. I doubt she left the party for even a second. It's not her he's covering for. There is someone else, though. And I'd put money on the fact that she is the murderer."

My brow crinkled as I wondered what I was missing. "Who?"

"Sonia."

"Sonia?"

"Yes, the woman he told Andrew to attend to before he vacated the castle. Sonia."

"We don't even know who Sonia is or what she means to him."

"She's the woman from the tower. It fits! The body falls from the tower. Randolph sent Andrew to the tower. The woman there murders him. When the investigation draws too much attention, Randolph confesses to divert the attention away from Sonia."

"That's a great theory, Cate, but it reminds me of a certain cheese."

"Huh?" Cate asked, her face a mask of confusion.

"Your theory is like Swiss cheese, it's full of holes."

Cate frowned at me. "It's a darn good theory if you ask me. And I love Swiss cheese."

"Come on, Cate. Think about it. Really consider what you're suggesting. To start, what is the motive? Why would Sonia, who we don't know is even the tower lady, kill Andrew? Could Sonia possess the strength it takes to inflict the injuries Andrew sustained? Even if she did, does she have the strength to toss his dead body out of a window? From what we saw of her, which was only a glimpse, I understand, she appeared to be a smaller woman. No larger than you. Do you think she could have beaten Andrew and tossed him from a window?"

Cate sighed and silence fell between us. Cate's points weren't invalid, but we didn't have enough evidence to conclude she was correct.

"There's something else," Cate finally said. "When I had my unfortunate incident with Andrew..."

My eyes widened at her statement and I interrupted her. "Unfortunate incident? Is that what we're calling it now?"

Cate bit her lower lip. "Sounded better than saying when Andrew almost drowned me," she said with a shrug. "Anyway, when the 'thing' happened, Andrew mentioned something about having a good thing going that he wouldn't let me ruin. Could that play into it?"

"A good thing going?" I repeated, trying to understand the statement. "As in his position at the castle, perhaps?"

"But how would I ruin that?"

"By telling Randolph he was rude and manhandled you."

"He'd kill me over that?"

"Who knows," I answered as I rubbed my sore eyes. Time travel took a toll.

"I'm tired, too," Cate said with a yawn. "We're spinning our wheels. We need dinner and a long nap!"

Mrs. Fraser pushed through the door, carrying Cate's dinner tray. "All finished with your estate business and ready for dinner, I hope!"

"Estate business is never finished," I responded as I stood with a groan.

"That's the truth, but time for a break. Now, come on, you," she ordered me, "let's leave Lady Cate to a quiet meal. She looks as though you've tired her out with all your estate business."

I left for dinner, hoping I could stay awake for it and the drive home. I had no trouble and even got to write this entire rather long entry. Despite my exhaustion, my brain is whirling with a replay of the events. I've come to no new conclusions about anything except one thing. I'm now almost entirely certain Randolph did not kill Andrew Forsythe.

CHAPTER 24

November 1
8:43 p.m.

I spoke with Cate after breakfast, and we agreed to return mid-morning to assess the situation in 1856. I arrived at the bedroom and found Cate dressed and waiting for me.

"You're early!" I said. I slipped into the closet and changed quickly before inviting Cate inside.

"Ready?" Cate answered.

"Anxious?"

"Yes. I won't deny it. I'm nervous. I feel sorry for Randolph and Victoria. Even if we learn nothing, we can at least support them."

"I understand. I feel the same way. Randolph didn't commit this crime. It is a shame his family is destroyed by this. I still can't figure out why he does it."

"Let's hope to get some answers today. Let's not push too much, though. I realize we only have a limited amount of time, but I think we should proceed with caution."

"Ohhhh, what's this I'm hearing? Lady Cate wants to proceed with caution? I can't believe my ears!"

"Oh, stop," Cate answered with a chuckle. "I'm being serious."

"I'll believe it when I see it, Cate. Now, come on."

We activated the timepiece and returned to 1856. After sneaking from the castle, Thomson ushered us into the house. He took us straight to Randolph's office. We passed two police officers as we entered.

"Jack, Catherine. Thank you for coming. Catherine, Victoria is in her room. She has not emerged from it. But I'm sure she would see you."

"I will visit her in a moment. Are there any developments regarding the investigation?"

"The officers told me they expect the autopsy to occur early next week. They're bringing in a coroner from Edinburgh. I don't understand what they expect to find. The man fell from a third-story window."

"Randolph, what did you discuss with the police yesterday?" Cate inquired.

"The standard questions, same as they asked everyone, I assume. My whereabouts, information about Andrew, any issues I've noticed as his employer."

"What did you tell them?" she continued.

Randolph's brow furrowed as he answered. "The truth. I told them I last saw him alive when I fired him. I imagine you overheard that. We then spoke for a few minutes before returning to the party."

"We weren't with you returning to the ballroom," I reminded him. "Did you tell them that? We did, I hope it hasn't caused any trouble."

"No trouble at all. I arrived in the ballroom only a few moments after you. I spoke with a few servants, then returned to the ball. They can confirm my story."

Cate glanced at me. This matched with the alibi disclosed in the early news articles prior to Randolph's confession.

"I'm glad. I have been worried all night. If you'll excuse me, I'll go to Victoria now," Cate said. She departed from the room, leaving me alone with Randolph.

"Please, sit," Randolph offered.

"Thank you." I eased into the seat across from Randolph.

He collapsed into his chair behind the desk. "Oh, what a terrible mess this is," he admitted. "Poor Victoria. I'm afraid she hasn't quite recovered."

"Have you?" I questioned.

He shrugged. "I am far better equipped for this than she. She isn't used to the rumors about the estate. Poor woman thought we may somehow escape them. That the castle could become a beacon of gentility rather than a source of gossip."

"There will always be rumors. It's people's nature."

Randolph nodded. "You're a smart man, Jack. I am pleased you've returned and hope you will continue. Catherine's presence soothes Victoria so."

"Catherine is most anxious to help Victoria," I assured him. "We will do our best to return until the situation resolves."

Before Randolph could reply, a knock sounded at the door. "Come in!" he called.

Malcolm opened the door and stepped inside. "Ah, Jack!" he said as he entered.

"Malcolm," I greeted him, standing and extending my hand to shake his. He shoved the rolls of paper he carried under his arm and shook my hand.

Malcolm glanced at Randolph as he continued into the room. "It's fine, both Jack and Catherine are intimately aware of the situation," Randolph informed him.

Malcolm nodded, and I noted an immediate change in his posture as his shoulders relaxed. "Terrible business,"

Malcolm said to me, his mouth drawn into a thin line. "I understand you were there when it happened."

"Yes," I confirmed as I regained my seat. "Randolph and I went out when the commotion began and spotted the body."

Malcolm sat next to me and shook his head. "Andrew was not the most congenial of individuals, but still his death leaves a shadow over the estate."

"He was a louse," Randolph responded from behind his desk. "He cast a shadow over this estate, alive or dead. Which is why I dismissed him. It's a terrible shame he didn't leave before he caused more trouble."

"Really, Randolph," Malcolm replied, "the man is dead."

Randolph waved his hand in the air. "Let us not discuss it further, he deserves no more of our time."

"With any luck, this nasty business will be concluded soon," Malcolm said. "Did the police give any indication earlier about that?"

"They are performing an autopsy on Tuesday. What they expect to find is beyond me," Randolph answered.

"Is it customary?"

"Yes, they implied it was. Though why they must bring a doctor from Edinburgh escapes me. Have we no doctors capable in the area?"

"Perhaps they hope to ensure an impartial party," Malcolm suggested.

Randolph threw his hands in the air and sighed. "This supposed desire for an impartial party is causing a lengthy delay in the process."

"I'd hardly call a few days lengthy," Malcolm countered.

"Any delay that causes my wife to suffer further is lengthy. I'd like the matter put to rest."

"With any luck, Tuesday will finish the entire horrid affair."

"From your lips…" Randolph said, allowing the rest of the

statement to remain unsaid. "Not to dwell on an unpleasant subject, but what did Andrew mean about asking Catherine about the lengths he would go to?"

My heart pounded faster as Randolph focused his gaze on me. I shrugged in an attempt to display nonchalance. "Andrew caught us on our way to the time rip. He was rather rude to us about it, threatened to make things uncomfortable for us if we continued to 'traipse' around the castle, as he put it."

Randolph's eyes narrowed at me. "That hardly warrants the statement he made."

"As you noted, he was a troubled man. He intended to threaten you into agreement is likely the case."

Silence fell over the room again. Randolph leaned forward in his chair after a moment. "Well, shall we change the subject to something brighter yet blander?"

Malcolm chuckled and shook his head. "One day, Randolph, I shall make you enjoy estate business."

"Oh, Malcolm, I do hope you are not very attached to that goal. I fear you may face only failure pursuing it."

Malcolm rolled a few papers across the desk. "Tell me, Jack, is Catherine this resistant to estate discussions?"

I chuckled. "She does not find it in any way pleasant or enjoyable," I admitted.

Randolph smirked and pointed at me. "A smart woman," he said. "I knew I liked Catherine for a reason."

"Come, Randolph," Malcolm prodded, "we must finalize these plans and begin to order materials for a spring start."

I stood to review the plans. "Now, I've incorporated Jack's suggestions," Malcolm continued, pointing out a few modifications.

My mind processed the conversation. Malcolm's water closet project was a major undertaking. Even from a modern perspective, bathroom remodels could be overwhelming.

Adding several to a castle of this size in the highlands was a tall order in the 1800s. The timeline struck me. Finalizing plans in November so an order for materials would be ready and on-site by spring!

We spent the next hour discussing and settling the final plans, much to Malcolm's delight. As we finished up, a knock sounded. Cate stuck her head in. "Sorry to interrupt, I'm just here to collect Jack."

I rose from my seat and said my goodbyes. Randolph inquired, "When can we expect you again? I hope soon."

"Tuesday," Cate answered, "for dinner."

"I shall look forward to it," Randolph answered.

We exchanged handshakes before Cate and I returned to the closet and our time. "Change and meet to discuss before lunch?" Cate questioned.

"Sure, meet you in the library," I responded.

As soon as I changed, I entered the hall with one destination in mind: the comfy armchair in the library. I slumped into it, enjoying the soft leather that surrounded me as I sunk down. I considered putting my feet on the coffee table, though decided I'd never hear the end of it if Mrs. Fraser caught me.

Cate arrived a few minutes later and sunk into the armchair next to me. She dove straight into our business.

"We can confirm that Randolph had a solid alibi now. If servants saw him after we did, there's no way he had time to kill someone and return to the ballroom."

"Right, so we have that confirmed."

"Nothing more to note on my end from Victoria. So far, she's holding up okay. It's taken a toll, but she's doing fine. I imagine the real issue will come when Randolph confesses. Perhaps we can avoid that."

"I don't see how. I've got nothing on my end. Randolph acts like nothing happened. He will barely discuss it. We spent most of the time discussing estate business. He asked about the circumstances of your mishap with Andrew."

"What did you tell him?"

"I danced around an explanation, saying Andrew caught us on the way to the time travel location and wasn't happy about it."

"Did he buy that story?"

"I think so, yes."

"Anything else?"

"No, nothing of note. Although can I just say how weird it is to discuss estate affairs with my great-great-great-grandfather?"

"No stranger than it is to discuss fashion with my great-great-great-grandmother," Cate said with a chuckle.

"You win. Estate business has changed less than fashion."

"Well, anyway, it looks like we're on hold until Tuesday, well Monday for us. I told Victoria we'd visit then, and she invited us to dinner. I'm hoping the autopsy results are in. That's when the real action begins. Until then, Randolph will tell us nothing."

"I agree. He's tight-lipped, and he will remain so until something precipitates a major change."

"Right, like him confessing to a murder he didn't commit to protect Sonia. I hope we can prevent that, but I'm not sure."

"We may have to let it play out. We're not supposed to be changing things, remember?"

Cate scrunched up her face. "Yes, I know. But I intend to prevent Randolph from going to jail and ruining his and Victoria's futures. I'm just warning you," she said, shooting me a glance.

"I realize that. I won't try to stop you. You're protecting your family. I'd do the same if it was Malcolm accused. Rules be damned."

The answer must have pleased her since she didn't argue. "Well," she said as she stood, "it looks like you're off the hook for the weekend."

"Oh boy," I answered as I rose from the comfy chair, "you mean I only need to go through forty-eight hours in the next forty-eight hours?"

Cate chuckled. "Yes, two whole days of only twenty-four hours each."

"What will you do with your normal twenty-four-hour days?" I winked at her.

"Fret, most likely," she admitted. "I'll try to keep my mind off things by working on my book and maybe getting a few things ready for Molly's arrival."

So, it looks like we're on hold for the weekend. There would be no additional information forthcoming until Monday. The only thing we know for sure is Randolph is innocent, and he is about to pay for a crime he didn't commit. So far, our presence in the past has done little to change anything.

CHAPTER 25

November 4

7:49 p.m.

e returned to 1856 around mid-afternoon. If the facts remained the same as they were in the newspaper articles, today would be the day everything changed for the MacKenzies of this era. The autopsy results would be revealed today, and Randolph would confess to a crime he didn't commit.

A bundle of nerves, Cate and I returned to the past and gained admittance to the castle. The moment we entered the foyer, I realized something was off. A heavy pall hung in the air. Victoria swept in. Her beautiful features distorted into a mask of worry.

"Thank God you're both here, cousins. Please, come quickly."

"What's happened?" Cate asked.

"It's terrible. The police are here speaking with Randolph. Andrew did not die in the fall. He was hit on the head, that's what caused his death. A blow to the head." She wrung her hands. "Well, blows. There were multiple. This has now changed the entire investigation. It's now considered murder. They are questioning Randolph further and want to search the castle. What a disruption. Oh, I am so sorry, we may be late for dinner."

"Don't worry about dinner, Victoria. I'm glad we are here to wait with you. Let's sit down."

"Oh, yes, let's sit down. Oh, Jack, you're an attorney, aren't you? Perhaps you could join Randolph in speaking with the police. I'd feel so much more at ease knowing you were there, that he had legal advice from someone we can trust, from family."

"Ah…" I hesitated. I had no experience with the law outside of watching a few episodes of an overly dramatic crime drama. I just needed a way to decline politely. Perhaps I could say criminal law was outside my expertise.

"He would be more than happy to," Cate answered for me as I pondered my response. She gave me an encouraging nod.

"Oh, thank you," Victoria said, leaping from her chair and throwing her arms around me.

"That's what family is for," I said with an uneasy laugh. "Catherine, a word before I join Randolph?"

Cate grasped Victoria's hands in hers before stepping away into the hall with me.

"Cate, are you crazy?" I whispered. "I'm not an attorney.

"No, but you're aware of the specifics of the case. You know where this is heading. The 'legal advice' is the easy part, tell him to remain silent! Just make sure he doesn't confess to a murder he didn't commit. And don't let them search the house without a warrant. You can stall them until we can brainstorm, just tell the police they aren't allowed to do what they want to do without a judge signing off."

"You watch too much *Law and Order*, Cate."

"Good thing I did!"

"Maybe you should be the lawyer," I suggested as I tugged at my collar, which suddenly felt far too tight.

"I can't, there aren't women lawyers yet, remember? Come on, you can do it! I have faith in you."

I nodded. "Okay, here goes nothing." I offered a salute before I headed down the hall to Randolph's office, where I assumed Randolph and the police were speaking. My suspicions were confirmed as voices floated down the hall as I approached.

My knuckles rapped on the open door, halting any conversation inside. "Jack!" Randolph said from where he stood behind his desk. "Come in, come in."

I stepped inside and nodded to the two officers. "Gentlemen," I greeted them.

"I suppose Victoria has passed along the news?" Randolph asked me. "It seems Mr. Forsythe did not die in the fall but rather, was murdered."

"Yes," I confirmed. "Terrible news."

One of the officers addressed me. "Excuse me, sir, but we must continue our conversation with Lord MacKenzie and prefer to do it in private. If you'll step out…"

I cut him off before he could finish. "I'll do nothing of the sort." I circled around them and stood near Randolph on the opposite side of the desk. "I am here in my official capacity."

"Which is what, sir?" the officer asked.

"Legal counsel for Lord MacKenzie."

"Legal counsel?" the officer questioned. His gaze flitted to Randolph. "Lord MacKenzie, you felt the need to summon legal counsel for this discussion? Are you hiding something?"

"Not at all!" Randolph started as I also spoke. "Absolutely not," I said. "Lord MacKenzie is my cousin, first off. Second, there are far more reasons legal counsel may be relied upon other than in the matter of hiding something.

The officer's eyes narrowed at us. "You are aware Andrew Forsythe's death was the result of several blows to the head?" he asked.

I nodded in response. "Lady MacKenzie informed me of the development upon our arrival."

"You understand… as a man of the law, this changes the trajectory of the entire investigation."

"Of course," I answered.

"We will be speaking with everyone again and we will be searching the castle," the officer informed me. "Before you arrived, we informed Lord MacKenzie he must provide full access to all areas…"

I held up my hand to halt his speech. "I'll stop you right there, sir." The officer cocked his head and furrowed his brow at me.

"You'll do nothing of the sort without the proper clearances. Have you a warrant?"

He swallowed hard and stared at me for a moment. "Well…"

"As I figured," I said, clasping my hands behind my back and pacing the floor. "You've no warrant. You are here demanding illegal access to this household to conduct a search that you've no right to conduct. Until you have the proper paperwork in place, you won't peek at a flower bush on this estate. Now, if there's nothing else…"

The officer set his face, his lips turning downward in a scowl. His face reddened as I spoke. "Lord MacKenzie," he spat at the end of my speech, directing his comment toward Randolph, "I'd suggest you cooperate with us as it will go much smoother that way."

"And I would suggest you cease threatening my cousin before I have a formal complaint drawn up against you," I retorted.

He glowered at me a moment before he spoke again.

"Fine," he said in a clipped tone. "We shall return WITH the paperwork you require. We will have our search, Mr. MacKenzie."

The man spun on his heel, signaling his partner to follow. They stalked from the room.

"Good show, Jack," Randolph said, clapping me on the back. He checked his timepiece. "We've delayed dinner, how tedious. Let us proceed and put this nasty business behind us."

I nodded, and we returned to the sitting room. Victoria rushed toward us. "What happened?" she inquired.

"They're gone for now," Randolph told her.

Cate stared at me. "They cannot search the castle until they have a warrant to do so. I expect them to return, but we will be prepared when they do. This will not be chaos, they will respect your rights and your home."

A smile spread across Cate's face and she winked at me.

"Thank heavens and thank you, cousin Jack," Victoria said, fanning herself as she collapsed into a chair. "What a mess."

"Indeed," Randolph agreed. "With any luck, it will be cleared up soon and we can return to our lives.

"Do the police have any suspects?" Cate asked.

"They haven't said," Randolph answered. "Andrew had several questionable associates, though. It doesn't surprise me this was his fate."

"Just terrible," Victoria said, shaking her head.

"Enough of this talk tonight," Randolph said, pouring a drink and handing one to me.

Victoria agreed. "We should go in for dinner, I imagine Cook is beside herself with the delay."

"Yes, I expect you are correct, my dear. Shall we?"

Halfway through our meal, Thomson whispered something in Randolph's ear. His expression clouded, and he whispered a response to Thomson, who disappeared from the room. Moments later, he returned and offered another hushed comment to Randolph.

Randolph grimaced and flung his napkin onto the table. "How dare they intrude on our dinner!"

"What is it?" Victoria asked.

"The damned police," Randolph said, standing. "They have sought Judge Darrow over his supper to obtain a warrant."

I stood also, prepared to follow Randolph to speak to the police. As we turned from the table, the doors burst open. Several police officers stormed into the room.

"What is the meaning of this? How dare you interrupt my meal!" Randolph shouted as they entered the room.

"Allow me to handle it, Randolph," I said, placing myself between Randolph and the officers. "May I see the warrant, please?"

One officer handed me the paperwork, adding, "You'll find everything in order. We shall begin our search posthaste."

"Just a moment." I held up my hand.

"Mr. MacKenzie, please stand aside and allow us to conduct our business. The warrant is in order."

"I…" I began. I scanned the papers as my mind worked to come up with an argument to prevent the search. Victoria joined Randolph, putting her arm on his shoulder. Cate glanced over my shoulder at the paperwork. "It appears everything is in order."

"Right, boys, let's begin!" the officer ordered.

"Just a moment!" Randolph shouted. "No one will lay one finger on anything in this house!"

"Lord MacKenzie, you must not interfere with this investigation, please stand aside."

"There isn't a need for a search," Randolph insisted.

"Do you have information that would suggest a search is not warranted?" the officer asked.

"Yes…" Randolph began.

My stomach somersaulted as I anticipated the chain of events about to unfold. "Wait, Randolph," I cautioned. "do not say another word." I turned to the officer in charge. "I'd like a private moment with my client."

"If your client has information about the murder, I'd like to hear it."

"And you shall," Randolph insisted.

"Randolph, please, I must insist as your legal counsel that you remain silent."

"Enough of this charade, boys, search the house."

"There's no need, I tell you! The murderer is right here. It was me. I am the guilty party. I killed Andrew Forsythe."

My head sunk to my chest at the admission. Behind me, Victoria gasped. Randolph, in a desperate attempt to stop the search of his home, confessed to a murder he did not commit.

"You?" the officer questioned the unexpected turn of events.

"Yes. I did it. I created a false alibi, but I can no longer live with the guilt."

"Randolph, please," I insisted in a desperate attempt to stave off any further incriminations.

Randolph waved me off. The police officer, eyes wide, shook his head, saying, "Randolph MacKenzie, I place you under arrest for the murder of Andrew Forsythe."

"Oh my God," Victoria exclaimed, swooning. Cate raced to her side, sitting her in a chair. One of the other officers handcuffed Randolph.

"I suppose you can lead us to the murder weapon," the lead officer asked. "Otherwise, we still must conduct the search."

"I can tell you where it is, but I doubt you'll find it. I threw it in the loch the day after the murder."

"We'll try dragging the loch tomorrow morning. It's too dark now," the officer said. "Come along, Lord MacKenzie, we need to take a formal statement from you at the station."

Cate leapt to her feet from Victoria's side. "Jack," she whispered, "you must go with him."

"What for?" I whispered back. "He IS a murderer, he's murdered any attempt I have at a defense!" I continued, my voice thick with sarcasm.

"Still! Go with him, try to minimize the damage. And try to find out why he's doing this!"

I sighed and nodded, "Okay, okay. I'll see what I can do."

"Good luck."

"I shall go with my client. He is not to be questioned unless I am present," I said, returning to my normal voice.

"Very well. You both can follow me," the officer said.

"Oh no!" Victoria cried, "Randolph!" She sprang from her chair, throwing her arms around him. "Please," she begged the officer, "please do not take him."

"Lady MacKenzie, please stand aside."

"No!" she wailed.

The officer nodded to another, who pulled her away. "Don't touch me!" she shouted.

"Get your hands off of my wife!" Randolph bellowed, approaching the officer. Chaos ensued as the police restrained both Victoria and Randolph.

"Victoria, please," Cate said, grabbing her by the shoulders, "this will not help. Please, let Jack straighten it out."

Tears fell from Victoria's eyes. "Yes," she gasped out. "Please, cousin Jack, help him." She flung herself into my arms, sobbing. I consoled her, promising to do my best. Cate pulled her away, sitting her in a chair while we cleared the room.

The officers led a handcuffed Randolph through the front entrance and into the waiting police cart. I climbed aboard with him and we set off for the rough ride to town. Despite the chilly night air, sweat beaded on my brow. The nightmare that waited at the police station loomed over me. I had no real legal experience. The altered newspaper articles would now report Randolph MacKenzie was convicted due to shoddy representation, I mused.

CHAPTER 26

November 4
9:54 p.m.

I pulled my jacket tighter against the night air as we rumbled into town and to the police station. The officers led us inside and to a small room with sparse furnishings. Still handcuffed, one officer pushed Randolph into a chair. I pulled another chair around the wooden table and sat next to him.

"I'd like a moment with my client," I said.

"We'll need to question him," the officer responded.

"I understand, but I'd like a word with him first."

The officer shrugged but relented. "We'll return in five minutes."

The door swung shut as he exited, and I turned my focus to Randolph. He stared ahead, unblinking.

"Randolph," I began. "You cannot do this." I received no response. "Think of Victoria and Ethan."

"I am thinking of them," Randolph responded.

"Randolph, Victoria is devoted to you, please. Retract

your confession. Tell them you were confused. We'll figure something out, but please, do not do this."

"You cannot change my mind, Jack."

"You mustn't do this. At the very least, remain silent, do not answer their questions until we can discuss this rationally."

Randolph did not respond. I hoped this was practice for his responses to the police. Two officers strode through the door moments later.

They took seats across from us at the small table. "Lord MacKenzie, you indicated you murdered Andrew Forsythe. Can you describe in detail your actions on 31 October that resulted in his death?"

"I'll stop you there," I interjected. "Lord MacKenzie…"

"We argued, I bashed him in the head, he died," Randolph interrupted with a shrug.

I closed my eyes in frustration. With every statement, the man insisted on incriminating himself for a crime he couldn't have committed. Why?

"What did you argue about?"

"I'd advise you not to answer," I said again.

Randolph shrugged. "A woman."

My brow scrunched as I pondered his meaning. Was he about to admit the truth of the matter? Did it relate to Sonia?

"What woman? What was the nature of your argument?"

"I accused him of having scandalous designs regarding my wife."

"Lady MacKenzie? You believed Andrew to be infatuated with Lady MacKenzie."

"It went further than that. Andrew had more than an infatuation. His salacious behavior even extended to our own dinner table."

"Randolph," I cautioned under my breath.

"Might you explain further?"

"No," I broke in, but Randolph spoke over me.

"The night before our ball, I noted a glance he offered my Victoria. Like a wolf, eyeing his prey. It infuriated me."

"But you waited until the following evening to murder him."

"I hadn't planned on it," Randolph responded.

"You hadn't planned to murder him?"

"No.

"So, what prompted you to?"

"While at the ball, I caught him ogling her again. I confronted him over it, dismissed him from his position."

"And then killed him?"

"Yes."

"Why kill him after dismissing him?"

"He was not pleased by his dismissal. He threatened to do… terrible things to Victoria. At the threat, I grabbed the nearest object and hit him with it."

"How many times?"

"Two."

One officer's head jarred up as he offered a quizzical glance at Randolph. "No, three," Randolph corrected.

"And then? How did he come to be outside?"

"I dragged him."

"You dragged a dead body through the castle halls and into the back gardens where he almost certainly would be spotted by a guest?"

"Yes," Randolph responded. "I did not care to hide the body to be dealt with later. I figured his death would be assumed a suicide, and the case wrapped up quickly."

"What did you grab?"

Randolph didn't respond. "What?" he questioned.

"What did you grab to hit Mr. Forsythe with?

"I don't recall."

The officers glanced at each other.

"Please, gentleman, that's enough for now," I said.

"All right," one responded. "We may have follow-up questions, but for now, we'll allow you some time to consult with your client."

They rose from their seats and left us alone in the room.

"Well, I'm glad that is over," Randolph mentioned after they departed.

"I am not. Randolph, as your legal counsel, I must advise you to cease speaking with the police and recant your confession."

"Why, Jack? I've killed a man. I'm doing the right thing, the noble thing."

"You didn't kill Andrew Forsythe."

"But I did, Jack."

I shook my head at him. "You didn't, Randolph. You couldn't have."

"Because I am incapable? I assure you I am more than capable of such a crime."

"No, because you simply did not have the time to kill him. You returned to the ballroom minutes after us."

"Plenty of time to commit the crime.

"You did not do this. It is impossible that you killed Andrew Forsythe. Randolph, stop this sham of a confession now before it's too late."

"I cannot fathom what else I may say to you, Jack. I remain steadfast in my decision."

I sighed and slouched in my chair. "I do appreciate your legal counsel in this matter, but I must be allowed to obey my conscience."

"Why are you doing this, Randolph?

"I have already explained it to you."

My waving hand stopped his speech. "Yes, I've heard your supposed reasoning. Why are you doing this? Who are you protecting? You couldn't have committed this crime, so who did? And what hold do they have over you to force you to confess to a crime you didn't commit?"

"I cannot answer any of those questions, Jack. All I can say is what I am doing is for the best."

"As your legal counsel, I must make my opinion abundantly clear. You should not do this, and you should allow me to handle the fallout now. You mustn't say anything further."

"I realize what I am doing, Jack," was his response.

I gave up. We were getting nowhere. We sat in silence for over an hour as we waited for the police to make their next move.

At long last, the door burst open. The two officers returned with several papers. They spread them across the table as they sat down. "Lord MacKenzie, we have several more questions…"

"Is this necessary?" I questioned. "My client has answered all your questions and described his story. Must you keep badgering at him?"

"Yes," one officer answered. "There are several of those details we need to discuss in greater depth. Your client has confessed to murder and we must build a case."

I grimaced, realizing I could not stop the questioning.

"Describe the timeline, again, Lord MacKenzie. At what time did you confront the deceased?"

"It was around nine-thirty, I believe."

"Can you be more specific?"

"No."

"Are you certain?"

"He's already told you to the best of his recollection the time, move on, gentlemen," I suggested.

"When we spoke with you on the evening of the murder, and you stated…" the man began as he shuffled the papers on the table. He found a specific notation and pointed to it. "You stated that you spoke with Andrew at approximately 9:30 p.m. During the conversation, which took approximately five minutes, you dismissed him from your employ, and he departed from your office. You spoke with Jack and Catherine MacKenzie following this before parting ways. You then spoke with three servants, Fiona, Thomas, and Elizabeth, regarding serving orders before returning to the ballroom. By your estimation, you returned to the ballroom around quarter to ten.

"Earlier this evening, you told us you killed Mr. Forsythe during your conversation. How did you accomplish this in the short time span you described to us?"

"I had plenty of time to commit the crime."

"In five minutes, you conversed with Mr. Forsythe, murdered him, dragged his body through the back halls and into the back gardens, then returned to speak with Mr. and Mrs. MacKenzie."

"No, I spoke with Andrew earlier than I told you. I had plenty of time to commit the crime."

The officer made a note on his paper before continuing. "And you said this altercation took place in your office."

"Correct."

"And you grabbed the nearest object to assault him."

"Yes."

"What was the item?"

"I do not recall."

The officer's eyes narrowed. "Really?" he questioned.

"It was a trying moment. No, I do not."

"Earlier you informed us you threw the murder weapon into the loch. How did you achieve this if you do not recall what the weapon was?"

I glanced at Randolph, awaiting his response to the officer's question. In preparing their case, they had noticed the inconsistency in his story. Perhaps all was not lost. Randolph swallowed hard before he set his jaw and spoke again. "I do not recall at this moment what it was, but I did recognize it after the murder. I disposed of it."

"When?"

"Right after the murder. The object was bloodied, I did not want anyone to discover it."

"Earlier you told us you disposed of it the day after the murder."

Randolph flinched but persisted with his tale. "Yes, of course. I am sorry, the situation disturbs me greatly, I am confused."

The second officer spoke up. "You also told us you created a false alibi regarding speaking with Mr. and Mrs. MacKenzie and your staff, but now you state you committed the crime before you spoke with them with ample time."

"I am uncertain of the exact times. I did create a false alibi. I spoke with Mr. and Mrs. MacKenzie, but I ordered the staff to lie about speaking with me to cover my tracks."

"You ordered the staff to lie so you could get away with murder?"

"Correct."

"Yet now you have confessed."

"I could not live with the guilt."

"Gentleman, that's enough for one night," I said.

"I'm afraid it's not, Mr. MacKenzie," the officer countered. "Lord MacKenzie has confessed to murder. After denying any knowledge of the crime. It is imperative we establish the exact details of the crime."

"Details that seem to allude you at the moment. Lord MacKenzie is in a highly emotional state given the current circumstances. He cannot process information clearly at the moment. I insist you cease badgering my client and allow him to rest before questioning him again tomorrow."

"We're hardly badgering, Mr. MacKenzie, and I prefer to

discuss the matter with haste. The further from the event, the hazier the memory."

"He has already told you what he recalls. How many times must he repeat it?"

"Until the details make sense."

"Or until you get the details you prefer to make your case easier."

"His stories contradict, and we must gain clarity."

"And you may gain it tomorrow."

"Fine," the officer agreed. "We will revisit the questioning tomorrow after Lord MacKenzie recounts his version one final time."

I shook my head at them but allowed them to proceed. Randolph recounted the events. "Around nine-twenty, I spoke with Andrew. We quarreled. I smashed his skull with the nearest object. I spoke with Catherine and Jack around nine thirty-five. Catherine and Jack departed, and I dragged Andrew's body to the garden below the tower, then returned to the ballroom. When the police arrived, I requested three staff members say they spoke with me, following my conversation with Catherine and Jack to establish an alibi. I removed the murder weapon the following day and threw it in the loch."

The police jotted down several things in their notes. "All right, Lord MacKenzie. We shall continue your questioning tomorrow."

"What time should we return?" I queried.

"We will begin questioning at 9 a.m. You may return before this to consult with your client if you prefer, Mr. MacKenzie."

"Lord Mackenzie will rest better in his own bed," I attempted.

"Lord MacKenzie murdered a man. I do not care where he would rest best. He will remain in our custody."

I nodded. "Randolph, I will return tomorrow morning."

Randolph nodded to me as one officer pulled him to standing and led him to a second door in the room. I sighed as the other officer directed me down the hall to the entrance. I checked the time as I stepped into the night air. My watch read just after twelve-thirty.

Weary with exhaustion, I began the walk back to Dunhaven Castle. Stars lit my path as I passed dark forms on either side of me upon leaving the town. Only dark blobs in the dim light, the trees swayed in the night breeze. I pulled my jacket tighter around me, wishing for the warmth a hoodie would provide. I normally found these clothes stifling, but tonight I could not shake the chill of the air.

Things spiraled downward in a matter of hours. Our presence had done little to change anything thus far. Events hurled toward the same outcome we'd read about in the newspapers. Soon, Randolph would be put on trial. He would be convicted and sentenced to death.

I could imagine the trial lasting only hours, his shabby excuse for an attorney beaten even with the inconsistencies in his statement. My feet stumbled across the gravel as I reached the castle's main drive.

Lights burned in several windows, despite the late hour. I took comfort in the stable structure. Despite my inability to protect Randolph, the castle would endure for centuries to come. And Lady Cate would arrive there in a little over one hundred and fifty years. The concept brought a smile to my face as I plodded past the front gardens and to the castle entrance.

I slipped inside through the open door without knocking. Thomson, out of his standard uniform and in nightclothes, approached me from the sitting room. The candle he held flickered as I shut the door, squeezing out the cool air.

"Mr. Mackenzie," he whispered.

"Thomson," I greeted him.

"What is the word? The entire staff has remained troubled by Lord MacKenzie's predicament. I offered to await your return."

"Lord MacKenzie remains in police custody and they will continue to question him tomorrow morning. For now, he is resting."

"Resting? There? Impossible!"

For the first time, I realized the depth of the man's commitment to the family. "I did my best to persuade them to release him, but I wasn't able to manage it. I am sorry."

"Oh, no, please, sir. I did not intend to impugn your work. I am certain you are using every tactic in your arsenal to help Lord MacKenzie."

And then some, buddy, I ruminated. I nodded at him. "There is nothing more tonight. Everyone should get some rest. I will collect Mrs. MacKenzie and we will return tomorrow."

"Oh, please, sir, allow us to prepare a room for you to stay. I am certain Lord and Lady MacKenzie would prefer it."

"Thank you, Thomson, though it is not necessary. We are not far. We will not trouble you."

"'Tis no trouble," he insisted, though I shook my head, cutting him off.

"No, no, it's quite all right, Thomson. Please, get some rest."

Thomson nodded. "Thank you, Mr. MacKenzie. We shall try to rest, though I would wager none of us will sleep a wink. Instead, we shall spend the night praying for Lord MacKenzie in this time of trial."

"I'm sure he will appreciate that very much," I responded.

"Mrs. MacKenzie is in Lady MacKenzie's suite. Miss Bryson is with them. She refused to leave, so Lady

MacKenzie will not be unattended if Mrs. MacKenzie departs."

I nodded to him and climbed the large stairway to the next level. I navigated to Victoria's bedroom and knocked lightly on the door. No response came. I tried again, but still nothing.

I eased the door open and peeked inside. Embers from a dying fire lit the room. I spotted Cate in an armchair near the fireplace. With her head titled back, she dozed in the chair.

I crept inside and knelt next to the chair. I gave her a gentle shake. Cate bolted upright, startled by the movement.

"Cate," I whispered.

"What? What time is it?" she asked, her voice groggy with sleep. Confusion flashed across her face before the realization of her whereabouts set in.

"Almost 2 a.m. You fell asleep. Come on," I said, standing and offering my hand for her to join me.

"Where are we going?" Cate asked, her voice still groggy.

"Home, silly."

"Home? What happened with Randolph? I should check on Victoria," she said, standing.

I stopped her. "Bryson is with her. We can talk about what happened when we get home and out of these clothes."

Cate nodded. Her brow remained furrowed, and she fought to regain all her senses. She glanced back toward Victoria's room. I pulled her toward the door, and we returned to the closet and slipped back to the present.

"Whew, what a night," I said when we were home.

"Yeah," Cate agreed. "I bet you are tired."

"You aren't kidding."

"Do you want to discuss everything tomorrow after you've had some sleep?"

"No. I'd rather do it while it's fresh in my mind. Besides,

I'll not be responsible for you lying awake all night wondering what's happened."

Cate gave me a small smile. "I appreciate that. I would like to know."

"Let's change. We have about thirty minutes before dinner."

"I'll ask Mrs. Fraser to send a tray up for you with mine, in the name of estate business. We can talk over dinner, then you can go home straight after."

"Perfect. I'll meet you in the usual spot?"

"See you in the library as soon as I'm changed and have taken the dogs for a quick pit stop."

I enjoyed the quiet lounge in the leather armchair as I awaited Cate's arrival. A few times, my chin touched my chest as I fought sleep.

Cate, her pups and Mrs. Fraser arrived. The smell of a warm meal perked me up a bit.

"Here we are, lazy bones," Mrs. Fraser joked, setting my tray in front of me.

"Thanks," I answered with a yawn.

"Now dinnae you go getting used to this treatment. I'm only doing it just this once," Mrs. Fraser warned.

I laughed. "I wouldn't dare, Mrs. Fraser, I wouldn't dare."

"I'm glad I did, I dare say you look like you're coming down with something!"

"Ah, I just didn't sleep well enough last night," I said.

"We'll see," Mrs. Fraser said. "Best you eat all your dinner and try to stave off whatever bug you caught. You sure you want to hang around this one, Lady Cate? I hope he doesn't breathe his germs onto you. Can't your business wait until you're well?"

"Afraid not. I won't breathe in her direction," I promised.

"Well, I suppose I'll go eat my own dinner far, far away

from the germs." Mrs. Fraser laughed, shaking her head as she walked away.

I dug into my meal.

"Hey," Cate chided, "stop breathing in my direction."

"Very funny, Lady Cate. You know very well I'm not sick."

Cate giggled before diving into her own meal. "Okay, so what happened? What took until two in the morning? And did Randolph come back with you? What did he tell the police? Is he sticking with his story?"

"Whoa, whoa, slow down, Cate," I said. "One thing at a time. I'll go over everything I remember, then you can ask questions."

"Okay," Cate answered, staring at me.

I took a few more bites of food before beginning. "Okay, so I tried my best, but Randolph is sticking to his story so far. I spent hours trying to talk him out of it, trying to find out why he confessed. I even told him we knew he couldn't have done it. He refused to change his mind. He refused to tell me who he was trying to protect. Kept saying he realized what he was doing, and he was guilty. I gave him my 'professional opinion' about what he was doing, he didn't care. The police questioned him. I did my best to minimize the number of questions and, after a while, they gave up. Told me they'd finish questioning him tomorrow. Speaking of, we need to be back tomorrow morning at nine for Randolph's questioning."

Cate nodded in agreement. "I don't get it. Why is he doing this? It has to be Sonia."

"He wouldn't say. What a mess. I fully expect to lose my first and hopefully only legal case."

"Well, your client isn't doing you any favors," Cate stated.

"No, he is not."

"How bad did the questioning go? What did he admit to?"

"Not much more than you already heard, thanks to my superb legal maneuvering. And what he explained fell short of making much sense. That's why the police want to question him again. And why I was able to postpone it until tomorrow."

"What do you mean?" Cate asked.

"The explanations he provided did not add up upon close inspection. He's lying, and it's obvious at times."

"Any specific discrepancies you remember?"

"He couldn't identify the murder weapon. Said he didn't remember what he grabbed to hit him with. When they questioned him on how he knew what item to throw into the loch, he flip-flopped, said he remembered what he hit him with at the time and directly afterward but can't remember now."

Cate raised her eyebrows. "That sounds made up. I remember the news story mentioned the police were skeptical. I'll bet this is why."

"There was another time they asked about his supposed alibi. He said he had time to commit the crime and talk with the staff. Later he said the staff lied on his behalf at his request."

"Is he still at the police station or did you get him out of custody?"

"I'm not THAT good of a fake lawyer, Cate," I said with a laugh. "No, he's still in custody. Will spend his night in a cell."

Cate shook her head at the situation. "Perhaps you'll have better luck tomorrow. I could speak with him, maybe that will help."

"It can't hurt. Although, we can't give him any information. You can't tell him what will happen to him or even hint at it."

Cate nodded in agreement. "You're right. But I can try to

convince him, anyway."

I nodded to her. "How is Victoria taking it?"

"Not great. I got her to sleep. Once she wakes up and finds out Randolph is still in custody, I can imagine it will send her into a tailspin."

"I would expect so, yes."

"I'm hoping my talk with Randolph kills two birds with one stone. Convince him to stop this charade and make sure he's okay so I can report back to Victoria and set her mind at ease."

"You're optimistic."

"I'm sure I'll fail at this, but I have to try to change this."

"Are you going to be okay if it turns out we can't?"

Cate paused, her brow furrowing in thought. "I'm not sure if okay is how I'd describe it, but…" She paused. "At least we tried. That's all we can do."

"I just don't want you upset over something that we very well may not have the power to change."

"I'm sure I'll be upset, but we have to try. If we can't change it, I'll accept that."

I wasn't certain if she was telling the truth, but at least her expectations were reasonable. "Well, that about does it for me. If you don't mind, I will head home."

Cate smiled. "I don't mind. Just leave that tray, I'll take it down with mine."

"And have Mrs. Fraser scold me tomorrow for making Lady Cate carry both trays? No way, lassie. I'll take them BOTH down myself. She's already mad at me for breathing my bogus germs on you."

Cate laughed. "Okay," she said, giving in, "you take them."

I gathered up the trays. Before exiting, I bowed extravagantly. "Good evening, m'lady."

Cate rolled her eyes, shaking her head and holding in a laugh. "Good night, Jack," she groaned.

CHAPTER 27

November 5
7:54 p.m.

ate and I traveled to the past early this morning. Randolph's questioning was scheduled for 9 a.m. I did not wish to be late for the disaster I was certain it would be, so we met at eight-fifteen and returned to 1856. Even with the walk to town, we arrived fifteen minutes ahead of time.

Cate informed me during our trek to town she desired to speak with Randolph. She had a practiced speech she hoped would convince Randolph to cease his foolish course of action.

After a bit of convincing on my part, the police allowed her five minutes with him. I waited in the lobby for her, whispering a silent prayer that she succeeded. After a few minutes, Cate appeared in the hallway.

"Any luck?" I asked.

Cate shook her head. "Afraid not. He wouldn't listen to anything I said."

"Great!" I said with a sigh. "Well, looks like I'm in for a fun morning."

Cate shook her head again. "Do what you can. I'll see you back at the castle."

"Be careful, Cate. Wish me luck."

"Good luck!" Cate said, giving my arm a squeeze. "You'll need it."

She pushed through the door, spinning to give me a wink and a wave before she disappeared into the November air.

I stalked down the hall toward the interrogation room. Randolph sat handcuffed at the table. I stepped into the room. The two police officers, named MacCrae and Abernathy, I'd learned, entered behind me.

"Gentlemen, may I have a few moments alone with my client."

"I'd like to get started, Mr. MacKenzie," Officer Abernathy replied.

"And I would like a few moments with my client to prepare."

"Prepare what? If he is being truthful, there is no need to prepare."

"I am not asking for anything uncommon. I'd like a few moments to discuss options with my client to ensure he is properly represented."

"Perhaps if your wife hadn't insisted on five minutes with Lord MacKenzie, you could have completed this," MacCrae retorted.

"My wife is visiting with Lady MacKenzie and hoped to take some news of Lord MacKenzie to her. It is not a surprising or inappropriate request. My client is cooperating in every sense. A little leeway is not too much to ask."

"Fine," Abernathy agreed with a scowl. "Five minutes."

They left the room, and I pulled a chair next to Randolph.

"I hope the night in your cell has brought some clarity," I began.

"If you mean have I changed my mind about proceeding with my admission of guilt, the answer is no."

I shut my eyes, steadying my nerves as I inhaled deeply. "Randolph, I cannot stress what a mistake this is."

"I have already heard the lecture from Catherine. A clever ploy, Jack, using my own progeny to sway me from my actions. However, not even charming Catherine can persuade me."

"It is not a ploy. Catherine is worried about you and the effect this will have on Victoria and Ethan. She meant every word she said, and she insisted on speaking with you. I had nothing to do with that."

"Either way, it has done nothing to change my position."

"Randolph," I tried one more time, "please. At least consult with an attorney with more experience in these cases. If you won't listen to me or Catherine, perhaps they can give you a better picture of what you are doing, or at least another option."

"I know full well what I am doing, Jack. I do not need another attorney."

"Damn it, Randolph, use some judgment here!"

"Jack, if you will not represent me in the manner I choose, I will dismiss you as legal counsel and do this on my own."

I sighed and rubbed my hand over my face. "Fine," I acquiesced. "But for the record, my legal advice is that you do not continue with this course of action."

"Noted," Randolph answered. "Now, let us proceed with today's questioning."

We waited for the two officers to return. "All finished, Mr. MacKenzie? Have we provided you with adequate leeway?"

I narrowed my eyes at him. This should be a fun morning, I surmised. "We are prepared to proceed."

"Wonderful," Abernathy said. They pulled chairs across from us and sat down. Officer Abernathy spread his notes across the table.

"Now, Lord MacKenzie, describe to us again the events of 31 October."

"Asked and answered," I retorted. I hoped to minimize any conversation on Randolph's part. If the glimmer of hope existed to get him out of this, I'd need him to have incriminated himself as few times as possible.

"And I am asking again," Abernathy answered.

Randolph spoke. "I left the ball to speak with Andrew…"

"At what time?" MacCrae interrupted.

"Nine-thirty," Randolph responded. "We spoke for a few moments. The conversation turned heated after I dismissed him from his post. We argued, and I grabbed the nearest object and hit him on the head."

"Your heated conversation," Abernathy said, "was regarding your wife, Lady MacKenzie, correct?"

"Yes. Andrew had been offering Victoria tawdry glances. I had caught him doing this over dinner the previous evening."

"What prompted you to discuss this with him at that moment?"

Randolph's brow pinched before he answered. "It occurred to me at that moment, and I wanted to address it."

Abernathy cocked his head to the side. "In the middle of your ball, you were suddenly struck by it and felt the need to confront Mr. Forsythe over a glance from the previous evening?"

"Yes."

"Why not confront him the evening before?"

Randolph shook his head and grimaced as he searched for

an answer. "I…" he began, then paused as he formulated his response. "I pushed it from my mind the night before. But it weighed on me. I could not convince myself it had been as trivial as I hoped."

"And you chose the middle of your first Halloween ball to speak privately about this with Mr. Forsythe? You were not busy attending to your guests? Or did not consider taking up a conversation following the party?"

"No, I wanted him gone from the house."

"In the middle of your party, you felt the urge to dismiss him?"

Randolph raised his eyebrows as though he recalled something. "No," he corrected. "No, he offered her another such glance during that ball. That prompted it."

"Ah, a second glance prompted it."

"Yes, yes, there was a second glance."

"And you took him aside into your office?"

"Correct. We stepped into my office. An argument ensued. And I hit him."

"You dismissed him. He argued with you, threatened Lady MacKenzie?"

"Yes, that's correct. The threat enraged me. I grabbed the nearest object and hit him."

"What was the object?" MacCrae inquired.

"I do not recall."

"You do not recall the weapon you used to murder a man?"

"No."

"Then how did you know what to throw into the loch the next morning?"

"I found an object with blood on it and assumed that was what I'd used."

"How many times did you hit him?"

"Two."

Abernathy ceased talking for a moment and raised his eyebrows. He shot a glance to MacCrae. He jotted something on his paper. "Two times."

"Three," Randolph corrected. "Three times."

"Is it two or three?" MacCrae snapped.

"Three," Randolph said.

Abernathy raised his eyebrows again before continuing. "And you still cannot recall the object?"

Randolph stammered. "Ah, it was… a… a weapon. A pistol."

"A pistol?"

"Yes. I keep one in my desk at all times. Heavy grip. It was my father's. Custom made. Terrible shame I destroyed it."

"All right," Abernathy said as he jotted another note on his paper. "You struck him three times with the butt of a pistol. Then what?"

"He fell over, and I realized he was dead. I dragged his body out of the room and to the back garden."

"And you did all of this within the span of five minutes?"

"Yes. No. No, it took me fifteen minutes to complete the task."

"And how did you speak with Mr. and Mrs. MacKenzie at nine thirty-five?"

"What?" Randolph questioned, his brow furrowing.

Abernathy consulted his notes. "Both you and Mr. and Mrs. MacKenzie informed us that you spoke around nine thirty-five. You said you spoke with Mr. Forsythe at nine-thirty. So, you had only five minutes to murder him and hide the body."

"No, I spoke with him earlier." Randolph paused. "Yes, earlier."

"How much earlier?"

"I spoke with him at nine-fifteen, yes, that's right, nine-fifteen."

"So, you killed him and disposed of the body before meeting with Mr. and Mrs. MacKenzie?"

"Correct."

"Yesterday, you told us you spoke with the MacKenzies then disposed of the body."

Randolph paused for a moment. "No, no, I moved the body first."

Abernathy scrawled a few more notes. "How were you not spotted by guests?"

"I was careful."

"Mr. Forsythe sustained injuries consisted with a fall. Do you know how he came to those?"

"I dropped his body when I transported it."

Abernathy narrowed his eyes at Randolph. "And after you spoke with the MacKenzies, you did speak with your staff? They did not, in fact, lie as you indicated yesterday."

"No, they are telling the truth. They did not lie."

"Why did you lie then?"

"I was confused. I'd forgotten."

"Were you aware of any business dealings Mr. Forsythe engaged in outside of his employ with you?"

"No," Randolph said with a shake of his head.

"Several of your staff reported witnessing conversations, some of them violent, with multiple individuals of... questionable character."

"I do not know anything about that."

"You were unaware of your employee's business dealings?"

"Completely."

"Are you quite certain?"

"He's answered the question, move on," I insisted.

"What are you getting at?" Randolph asked.

"I am suggesting, Lord MacKenzie, that this murder goes well beyond a fleeting glance at your wife. I am suggesting you were involved in a nefarious business deal gone wrong, perhaps, and this is the true source of the crime."

"How dare you, sir?" Randolph hollered. "I have no knowledge of any such dealings and certainly no involvement in them."

"Only an involvement in murder, is it?" MacCrae retorted.

"That's enough," I answered. "Enough questioning, enough badgering my client."

"We are not badgering, Mr. MacKenzie. We are merely trying to get to the truth."

"The truth is, I killed Mr. Forsythe. That is all you must know."

"Truth or not, Lord MacKenzie, you've given us conflicting information on multiple occasions. We cannot help but think there is more to the story."

"There is not," Randolph insisted.

Abernathy and MacCrae stared at him a moment longer. "All right, Lord MacKenzie," Abernathy said after a moment. He gathered his papers from the table and stood, tapping them against the wooden top. "Thank you."

"Wait just a moment," I said as both officers stepped toward the door. "Are you formally charging my client? Or may he go?"

"No, Mr. MacKenzie, he may not go. He is here under suspicion of murder. He cannot simply walk out of the police building and go about his merry way."

"Are you charging him?" I asked, unimpressed with the boorish behavior.

He hesitated a moment. "Not just yet," he answered after a time, then spun on his heel and disappeared from the room. MacCrae followed behind him.

I let out a long breath. I had no clue how to proceed. There was no use talking to Randolph about changing his mind. It appeared the questioning had ceased for the moment. Perhaps I should touch base with Cate, I mused.

"I'm going to head to the castle, fill Catherine in," I murmured to Randolph.

"Fine," he answered.

"Do not speak to them without me being present," I cautioned. Randolph didn't respond. "Do you understand, Randolph?"

"I do not see what difference it makes…"

"Don't," I interrupted him, "speak with the police without me. Please. I've let you sabotage your defense enough already. Please promise me this."

"I promise," Randolph agreed.

"Good."

I left the room and traveled to the entrance. An officer stood at the front desk. "Can you ask Officer Abernathy if he plans to question Lord MacKenzie further today?"

The man nodded and disappeared. Officer Abernathy returned with him. "You may go, Mr. MacKenzie. We will not be speaking with Lord MacKenzie further today."

"And will you be charging him?"

"If we charge him, we will inform you."

"Send any notice to the castle, I shall be there."

He nodded to me. With nothing left to do, I departed, stepping into the November air. Dunhaven Castle rose on the hill in the distance. I dreaded the discussion with Cate, though perhaps she would improve my mood.

I set off toward the castle. When I arrived, Thomson ushered me into the foyer. "Is there any news?" he questioned.

"None good. I must speak with Mrs. MacKenzie."

"I see," Thomson murmured, his lips pursing after his statement. "I shall fetch Mrs. MacKenzie, though I prefer Lady MacKenzie remain unaware of your visit. She will undoubtedly demand a report. If the news is not good, she may become further disturbed. She has made such strides since Mrs. MacKenzie arrived this morning. I would very much hate to disturb the progress."

"I see. If you could find a way discreetly to arrange a meeting with Mrs. MacKenzie, I would be grateful. It is important I speak with her. Though I, too, prefer to avoid Lady MacKenzie for the reasons you stated." The truth was, I did not want to face her with the news.

"Very good, sir. I shall do so at once. I have a way. Please wait here."

Thomson disappeared down the hall. I waited in the foyer, my throat dry, hoping Thomson's plan worked. I could not imagine informing Victoria of Randolph's predicament. I imagined her collapsing to the floor as tears fell to her cheeks.

Within a few moments, Cate appeared, hurrying down the hall, a baby balanced on her hip. The irony of Cate holding her great-great-grandfather struck me.

"Oh, Cate, I hope Thomson was discreet," I said as she approached.

"He was. Victoria is distracted, let's talk in the library."

We hurried down the hall and I closed the doors behind us after we entered the library. "What's happened?" Cate asked.

"It's not good, Cate. I mean, it's not terrible, but it's not good." Cate stared at me, waiting for me to continue. "The questioning did not go well. He's giving conflicting information, contradicting himself."

"That's not good."

"That's the good news," I said with a sigh. "His conflicting information has the police unsure. They haven't charged him yet, but I'm not sure how much longer we can avoid it. I'd guess a formal charge is coming this afternoon, tomorrow morning at the latest."

Cate sighed, her shoulders sagging. "We need a plan."

"You aren't kidding, one that is Randolph-proof."

"What do you mean?" Cate asked, her brow furrowing.

"He's impossible. I suggested he consult with a more experienced attorney in these types of cases before plowing ahead with his admission of guilt."

"And?"

"And he flat-out said no. Then threatened to fire me if I didn't do what he wanted." I rolled my eyes, recalling the ridiculous conversation.

"I cannot believe he is being so stubborn! How frustrating," Cate said, shaking her head. "How are you holding up?"

"I don't know. It is incredibly frustrating, but then again, I'm making this up as I go. I feel like I live on a bad episode of a legal drama."

"What now?" Cate asked.

"Unless he's charged, there's not much."

"Do you need to return to the police station?"

"There's no need for me to return today, but I'm not sure I want to face Victoria. Thomson seemed to think the mere sight of me may cause a fit."

"She is doing better than when I arrived this morning, but yes, Thomson may be right. I'm afraid the slightest thing will send her reeling."

"Ah, what a mess. Can't he see what this is doing to his wife?" I asked, throwing my arms in the air in frustration.

"Why is he protecting this other woman at Victoria's expense?" Cate sighed. She pursed her lips as she brooded. After a moment, Cate's gloomy expression changed, her eyes becoming bright, her lips parting in excitement. "Jack! Do you suppose you could go to the station and make sure they don't charge Randolph until tomorrow morning at the earliest?"

My brow pinched as I considered her request, more specifically as I considered the reason behind her request. "I'm not sure I can pull that off, but I can try. Why?"

"I have an idea. It would require us to return this evening, but I have an idea."

I was about to question the idea when Thomson knocked, then entered the room. "Pardon the interruption, but Lady MacKenzie is finishing up with Cook. Perhaps you should return to the solarium, Mrs. MacKenzie."

"Thank you, Thomson," Cate answered. Thomson nodded then exited, closing the doors behind him. "I'd better go."

I nodded. "I'll do what I can at the police station, then come back for you. Cate, I'm not going to like this idea you have, am I?"

"Not one bit."

"I was afraid of that," I said. "Can't wait to hear it so I can really detest it. Wish me luck!" I saluted to her as I strode from the room.

"Good luck!" she called after me.

CHAPTER 28

November 5

9:13 p.m.

I darted out a side entrance to ensure I would not run into Victoria and began my walk back to town. When I reached town, my muscles tensed, and my palms turned sweaty. I dreaded this task, but I would try my best. I hoped Cate's plan worked, though without understanding any details, I couldn't make any assessments. I could only do my part, which was to convince the police not to charge Randolph before tomorrow morning.

I pushed through the entrance and approached the clerk at the desk. "Excuse me, could I speak with Officer Abernathy?"

The clerk disappeared and returned with Abernathy. "I haven't charged him, Mr. MacKenzie."

"No, I realize that," I began.

"So, what is it now?"

"Will you be bringing formal charges against my client?"

"I am studying the evidence and making a determination. Once I know, I shall inform you."

"Could you wait until tomorrow to make your decision?"

"Excuse me?" he questioned.

"Wait until tomorrow. You said you're still weighing the evidence. Could you take another night's sleep on it and make your final decision tomorrow?"

His brow furrowed and stared at me. "What are you trying to pull here, Mr. MacKenzie?"

"I'm not attempting to pull anything over on you. I promise. But I have some rather urgent business and will not be able to represent my client fully until tomorrow morning."

"That is not my issue, Mr. MacKenzie. If I feel Lord Mackenzie should be formally charged, I must do so."

"I am not asking you not to charge him, merely to wait until such time as I can be present to represent my client fully. You should use the time to consider carefully the evidence. Lord MacKenzie very clearly is not thinking straight. You have questioned him multiple times because his accounts have differed."

"Just because he is a liar, Mr. MacKenzie, does not mean he is not a murder."

"You should consider other suspects. You already suspect he may not be guilty. It can't hurt to take some extra time."

His brows knit together tighter as he considered my request. "I..." he began before his voice trailed off.

"I'm not attempting to circumvent the law. I'm only asking for twenty-four hours. You said you weren't sure. Give me until tomorrow to conduct my affairs and I shall return tomorrow morning for your decision."

I received no response. I continued, "Look, Officer Abernathy, your department has barely conducted an investigation here. You've overlooked multiple suspects, made questionable decisions and taken the easy route at every turn. A formal charge without the proper amount of evidence will ruin your case before it's even begun. I urge caution on your part not only for Lord MacKenzie but for your own department. How embarrassing for you to botch this investigation."

He sniffed before rendering his decision. "Fine, fine, Mr. MacKenzie. I shall not charge him until tomorrow. But you had better be prepared then, and there'd better not be any further stall tactics."

"I promise you, sir, there will not be."

"Good day then, Mr. MacKenzie."

"Thank you and good day."

I stepped into the November sunshine and squinted up at the blue sky. White clouds sailed past but failed to obscure the sun. I set off to return to Dunhaven Castle with a spring in my step. To be honest, I couldn't believe that worked! I, Jack Reid, convinced the police not to charge Randolph before tomorrow. As much as I would likely hate Cate's plan, we had to make it work. My hard work had to pay off!

I hurried back to the castle, eager to learn the details of Cate's plan. Thomson greeted me at the door and showed me into the foyer.

"Mr. MacKenzie, any word?"

"Randolph will not be charged today," I said, choosing to lead with the good news.

"Wonderful news!" Thompson said. "The ladies are finishing their luncheon. I shall announce you."

My strategic plan did the trick. This time he'd allow me to speak with Victoria.

He disappeared down the hall and returned within moments. "Right this way, sir," Thomson said. I followed him to the dining room. As I entered, Cate's eyes fixed on me. I gave her a slight nod. She breathed a visible sigh of relief.

"What news of my husband?" Victoria inquired as I entered the room.

"The police have questioned him extensively. There will be no formal charge made for at least the next twenty-four hours."

"Will he be returning home?"

"Not yet. But I hope soon," I answered her.

"This is good news, Victoria," Cate said, placing her hand on Victoria's arm.

Victoria didn't look convinced but nodded her head at Cate, placing her hand over Cate's.

After a moment, she turned to me. "Have you eaten anything?"

"No, ma'am," I said, sitting down across from her.

"Oh, let me have something sent up. You must be famished!"

Cate smiled at me as Victoria rang for service. It seemed Victoria was returning to her old self a bit. I hoped whatever plan Cate had could ensure the trend continued.

Victoria requested sandwiches for me. I must have looked like an animal eating them. I was starved after the long, stressful morning.

"Thank you, Victoria. Those were excellent after my long morning. And I'm sorry to seem ungracious, but I have a few things I must attend to. Catherine, we should go and allow Victoria a chance to rest."

"Oh, must you go?" Victoria asked.

"I'm afraid we must," I answered. "We'll be back bright and early tomorrow morning, I promise. There is nothing we can do right now, Victoria. Please try to rest, this will all be over soon." I placed my hand over Victoria's.

Victoria clasped my hand in hers, also reaching for Cate's. "Thank you, both of you."

"Jack's right, Victoria," Cate said, "you should rest. This is taking a tremendous toll on you. Please promise you'll rest."

"I shall try," Victoria promised. "Although, I worry about Randolph. I do wish he was home."

"I tried my best…" I began.

Victoria waved her hand in the air, stopping me. "I understand and appreciate all that you've done. I'm not suggesting there is a deficiency in your work, Jack. But I would be more settled with Randolph at home. Still, I promise to rest."

"Good. As Jack said, we'll be here tomorrow morning."

"Let me ring for Nanny to take Ethan."

"Oh, let me take him to the nursery. We'll show ourselves out afterward."

"Are you certain?" Victoria asked. Cate nodded. "Thank you, Catherine. I shall see you tomorrow." Victoria embraced me then Cate, giving Cate a kiss on the cheek.

Cate and I returned Ethan to the nursery, then used a discreet path to get to the closet and return home. I breathed my customary sigh of relief after we were back.

"I'm dying to know how you pulled off your legal coup," Cate exclaimed after we returned.

"And I'm dying to know your plan to save a man who doesn't want to be saved," I answered.

"Meet in the library?" We said in unison.

Cate laughed. "Yes, after we change, of course."

"Of course," I responded with a chuckle.

I changed clothes and meandered to the library. I collapsed into my new favorite armchair and waited for Cate. Riley announced her arrival. He bounded in and stood on his hind legs as I ruffled the fur on his head. Bailey followed behind with Cate.

"Hey, buddy!" I exclaimed as Riley bounded over to me. "I missed you! Did you miss me?"

"I expect he did, despite us only being gone for..." Cate checked her timepiece. "Twenty-four minutes."

"This time differential is killing me. I've eaten lunch already, and it's only 9 a.m."

"I know the feeling." Cate sunk into an armchair. "Okay, I can't take any more suspense. How did you pull off the delay in the formal charges being filed?"

"I threw everything I could at them. Told them he was under duress, tired and not thinking straight. I reminded them that his story did not add up, and they needed to consider other suspects because of that. Then I threatened them about a few procedural things and they agreed to hold off."

"Wow, you must have been doing your homework. Been watching *Law & Order*, huh?"

"Yep," I said with a laugh. "Okay, your turn. I'm dying to learn how you plan to fix this."

"Randolph will not cooperate, we know that. So, it's on us to take matters into our own hands."

"I'm alarmed already," I admitted.

"We need to learn more about Sonia, about what motive she may have had and why Randolph would go to such lengths to protect her. Randolph isn't going to offer us any information."

"So, what do you propose we do? Give him truth serum?"

"No," Cate said, shaking her head. "I propose we ask Sonia."

"Ask Sonia?!" I exclaimed.

"Yes. Assuming she hasn't run away yet, she should still be in the tower room. We must ask her who she is and what happened that night. She must have killed Andrew. He fell from the tower, or so it appeared. He must have been with her and she must have killed him. We have a key. We'll take it back this evening, speak with Sonia, learn what we can and come up with a plan to proceed."

"What makes you assume she'll talk to you?"

"We must convince her. I think she will."

"Why would she? How are you so sure?"

"Well," Cate conjectured, pausing a moment, "she only has contact with the servant or servants who care for her. Randolph is gone. It was clear she was fond of him. She's got to be reeling, just like Victoria. Only she has no support system like Victoria has. The servants cannot provide her with any help, they have no means to. She may be more accommodating than we expect."

"It's a gamble."

"There isn't much choice."

"You're right. You want to do this tonight?"

"I think it may be best. Perhaps we can sneak back when most of the household is quiet. Then we'll have some time before we return tomorrow to sort through whatever information we receive and devise a plan."

"Okay, agreed."

"Wow, that was easy!"

"You make a good point. And my legal skills leave a lot to be desired. With Randolph's reckless behavior, he will go to jail. I can't stop it unless we gather more information. I don't want to be responsible for ruining Randolph's life."

Cate leaned forward and grabbed my hand. "You wouldn't be responsible, even if we can't stop this. Randolph is calling the shots. There's not much you can do."

"Thanks, Cate. But I still can't help but feel somewhat responsible, considering I am the man's legal counsel."

"I'm sorry about that. I feel terrible having put you in that position."

"Don't. I could have refused, but I wouldn't have."

"We didn't have to use the cover story we did. That's what thrust you into this position."

"I'd still be in this position. He refuses to have any legal counsel. He's only accepting my help because it would seem awkward to Victoria if he didn't accept 'cousin Jack's' help."

Cate smiled at me. "Thanks for being a good sport about it."

"No problem, Lady Cate. Now, I suppose some work awaits me."

"Maybe you should rest first? Catch a nap?" Cate suggested.

"I'll be all right. I'll take a quick nap after dinner before we travel back tonight."

"Sounds good. See you later… around eight?"

"Perfect. See you then, Cate."

I spent the rest of my day on pins and needles awaiting our next trip. I hated this plan, too much could go wrong. Yet, we had no choice in the matter. Without any help from Randolph, we didn't have a snowball's chance in… well, you know.

After dinner, I considered driving home for a nap, then returning. I figured Lady Cate wouldn't mind if I sneaked into the library and napped in one of my favorite armchairs. I slipped into the large space and dropped into the chair nearest the fireplace. Embers still glowed there from earlier in the day. The warmth lulled me into sleep.

I woke just in time to change and meet Cate. We slipped back to 1856 and tiptoed through the halls to the tower stairs. As we approached the top, my nerves got the better of me. "Are you sure about this?" I whispered.

"We don't have a choice. There are things we must learn, and confronting Sonia is the only way we will learn them."

"You're one brave but stubborn lassie, Cate."

"I will take that as a compliment. Let's go, before I lose my nerve."

We finished our climb. Cate inserted the skeleton key into the lock and turned it. I held my breath as the door swung open.

The tower room in this time housed a bed, dresser, writing desk, easel and a large area rug. Candles lit the room. Black fabric covered the windows.

A woman crouched at the large wardrobe that remained in the space in our time. She twisted to face us. She was younger than I expected. Dark hair hung around her pale face and blue eyes.

"Who are you?" she demanded.

Cate stepped inside and pulled me with her. She shut the door behind us. "We're friends of Randolph's. I'm Cate and this is Jack. Jack is representing Randolph in the case the police are building against him for the murder of Andrew Forsythe. Sonia, is it?"

The woman's forehead scrunched, and she bit her lower lip. "Will he be cleared of the charges?"

"That is our goal, but we need your help," Cate said.

"My help?"

"Yes. You must tell us what really happened that night," Cate urged.

She wrung her hands and bit her lower lip. The woman turned her back to us. "I do not know what you mean," she said.

"Sonia," Cate chided, "we don't have time for evasive answers. If we don't have the facts, we cannot help Randolph. Sonia, he'll go to jail! You don't want that, I know it." Sonia collapsed onto the bed, tears falling from her eyes. Cate continued, "Sonia, please help us!"

Sonia wiped the tears from her cheeks, composing herself. "How do I know I can trust you?"

"We're here to help, both you and Randolph. We realize Randolph has been protecting you, both by keeping you in the tower room and by confessing to a crime he didn't commit. What we don't understand is why. We need to understand that to help him." Sonia remained silent. "Sonia, please. Right now, we are your only friends. We only want to help. By the looks of it, you need it. Were you running away? Randolph will be devastated to find out you're missing."

Sonia nodded her head. "I must go. I've cost this family too much now."

Cate approached her, sitting next to her on the bed and putting her arms around her. "Sonia, Randolph will be devastated if you leave. We can help, but we must have all the facts. Please, help us help you and Randolph."

"Please," Sonia responded, "you mustn't tell anyone about me. Only Uncle Randolph and a handful of people know I'm here. Not even his wife Victoria is aware."

Uncle Randolph, my mind questioned? I hoped Cate picked up on it. Cate glanced at me with her brows knit. "Uncle Randolph?" Cate questioned.

Sonia wiped tears away. "Yes, Randolph is my uncle."

"Are you Lorne's daughter?" Cate asked, her confusion apparent.

"No, Emilia was my mother," Sonia said.

Emilia, I pondered? Who was Emilia? That name seemed familiar. After Cate continued, I recalled Emilia was Randolph's younger sister.

"Emilia?" Cate said. "She died from influenza at age fifteen. I wasn't aware she was married nor had any children."

"I'm afraid that's the story created to hide me, the ugly blemish on the family name."

"You mean..." Cate began.

"Yes, my mother died at age fifteen but not from

influenza, she died in childbirth. I was a bastard. She was unmarried. My grandparents preferred that I be an orphan. Although that's a far bit better than my paternal grandparents wanted for me. Uncle Randolph wouldn't allow it. He insisted I stay here, argued with his parents. They couldn't explain the new baby without questions being asked. My father's family wanted no parts of me, nor any potential for scandal on the family name. Uncle Randolph kept me a secret. Oh, please don't judge him for putting me in this room. I've been more than comfortable."

"I understand, and we will say nothing, but you must promise not to leave. We can make sure you remain safe. Now," Cate said, stroking her hair, "can you tell me what happened the night Andrew died?" Sonia wept again. "Shh, shh," Cate soothed her, "I realize how hard this must be, but we need to understand the facts so we can help you both."

Sonia nodded again, breathing deeply, composing herself. "Andrew used to bring me some of my meals. He was a vile man. Accused me of being many vulgar things. He blackmailed Uncle Randolph. At first, he paid, but Andrew demanded more and more. I felt so terrible. I almost left then; I wish I had."

"I'm sure Randolph is pleased you didn't leave."

"I do not agree," Sonia sobbed.

"It's all right, Sonia," Cate said, rubbing her arm, "please, continue."

"That night, that horrible night," Sonia lamented, "Andrew came here. He seemed different. Worse than ever, angry and bitter. He... He..." Sonia stumbled, unable to find the words. "He attacked me," she managed, a few more tears rolling down her cheeks. "He ripped my dress. Said that he'd have his way with me, too, like Randolph." Sonia choked out her words amidst tears, struggling to tell the story. "He..."

"We understand, Sonia," Cate assured her. "You then

defended yourself?" Cate asked, prompting her to move forward in the story and allowing her to skip rehashing any vile details she may not wish to relive.

She nodded, regaining her composure. "Yes. I grabbed the first thing my hand reached and hit him." Her shoulders sagged, and she sobbed as she continued. "I hit him. I hit him over and over until he didn't move."

Cate held her closer. "It's all right, Sonia. It's over now. You did what you had to do."

Cate glanced at me and I shook my head at her. That disgusting pig of a man, Andrew, deserved every blow he received that night in my estimation.

After a moment, Cate prodded her to continue. "How did Andrew end up falling from the window?

"Anna, one of the maids who has always been a loyal friend to me, helped me throw his body over. I didn't know what to do. I did not want Uncle Randolph to see what I had done. Perhaps he would have regretted his choice to help me. We struggled but succeeded in pushing him out the window nearest to this bed. I hoped it would appear as an accident. As though he had jumped. Then Anna assisted me in cleaning up the... mess. When Uncle Randolph told me the police were involved, I prayed they would find it to be an accident. But now..." her voice trailed off again.

"I don't want you to worry, Sonia. We're here to help."

"I don't see how," Sonia said, but regained herself a bit.

"Leave that to us. Can we trust you not to leave?"

"I imagine it would be easier if I did," Sonia argued.

"It wouldn't. Randolph will never forgive himself. Please promise us you'll stay, at least until you speak with us again."

Sonia nodded, "I promise. I will stay... for now."

Cate nodded. "Sonia, before we go, is there anything else you can tell us about Andrew that might help us?"

Sonia reflected for a moment. "Andrew was not a nice

man. He was involved in many nefarious things. I often spied him meeting with a man, exchanging things in the middle of the night. I am not aware of what the exact nature of their business was, but I cannot imagine it was anything respectable being conducted in the wee hours of the morning."

"Thank you, Sonia. That is helpful. I apologize for making you relive that night, but I assure you things will improve."

"Thank you for trying to help. And thank you for not judging my past."

"Try to rest, Sonia. We'll visit again when we have a solution."

"Please let it be soon," Sonia said.

Cate helped the girl remove her tattered cape and settled her in bed. She blew out the candles that lit the room before we snuck from it. She shut and locked the door behind her before we returned to the closet and our own time.

"That poor girl," Cate declared upon our return.

I shook my head again, disgusted by the ugly details. "And that bastard Andrew."

"Yes. We must come up with a solution. We have to help them!"

"I'd love to, I don't know how we can, though. I'm at a loss. Unless we turn her in for it and hope we can prove self-defense, I don't see a way out of this."

"There must be a way," Cate contended. "I need time to deliberate. Perhaps we should discuss this after breakfast and see if we have any solutions."

"Good idea," I said with a yawn. "Despite all the excitement, I'm exhausted. I don't think I can put an idea together. It's cutting it close though, I have to be at the station by tomorrow afternoon. They will charge Randolph, there's no avoiding it."

"Okay." Cate squeezed my arm. "Don't worry, we'll find a way. Try to get some rest. Are you okay to drive home?"

"Yeah, yeah, I can make it," I answered. "Hey, you try to get some rest, too. Don't be up all night scheming."

"Who, me?" Cate laughed. "Never! See you tomorrow."

"Yes, you, Lady Cate. Okay, see you tomorrow."

So, there you have it. We now know who killed Andrew and why. How it helps us escapes me. We can't provide Sonia as a suspect. We're at as much of a loss as we were before we understood the full circumstances.

I am exhausted, which isn't helping. I can't see a way forward. All this work for nothing? It seems that may be the case. Randolph may still pay for a crime he didn't commit.

CHAPTER 29

November 6
8:24 p.m.

Despite the hopelessness I felt last night, Lady Cate managed to turn that around this morning. Following breakfast, she popped into the kitchen, earning the wrath of Mrs. Fraser, who scolded her for carrying her tray downstairs.

Cate requested to see me about estate business. A part of me wondered if Cate really wanted to speak about estate affairs, though the larger part of me knew better. I followed Cate to the library.

She shut the doors behind us and grinned at me. "I have a plan!"

"Great! I came up with nothing, so I'm all ears. I can't believe it, but I'm all ears for a Cate Kensie plan."

"Keep an open mind. I don't have all the quirks worked out, but I think it might work."

"The only way Randolph will recant his confession is if

Sonia cannot be connected to the murder and there is no danger of her being found."

"Right," I concurred.

"Okay, so we need to make sure Sonia is protected. This will ensure Randolph's cooperation."

"How do we do that? Let her run away like she wanted to?"

Cate shook her head. "Nope. We let her live her life at Dunhaven Castle."

I furrowed my brow. Sounded like Cate had too little sleep and was talking in circles. "How?"

Cate grinned at me a moment before she explained. "You are Randolph's cousin. At least that's what everyone thinks. We'll pretend Sonia is your niece, which makes her related to Randolph through you. We tell everyone Sonia's parents died. But with the amount of traveling your law practice requires, it's impossible for us to take Sonia in. We ask Randolph to do it. I'm certain he'd be more than happy to, which is what he'll tell Victoria. Sonia gets to live a full life. Randolph stops his nonsensical behavior, and he doesn't go to jail for a crime he didn't commit."

I sunk into the armchair behind me as I processed the plan. "Do you imagine people will buy it?"

"It's 1856!" Cate exclaimed. "We can say Sonia's mother, your sister, died in childbirth, a very likely story and true. Her father raised her but was killed in an unexpected accident. It would explain why you insisted we leave yesterday."

I recalled my story to the police about my urgent business. Yes, this would fit very well.

"Okay, so how do we make this work? Do we just get Sonia from the tower room? How do we tell Randolph?"

"We'll have to move Sonia from the tower, yes. We'll make it look like no one has lived there, just in case. We'll tell

Randolph she's safe and the new plan. After that, he'll likely agree to recant his statement. That's where this gets tricky."

"What if they don't accept that?" I questioned.

Cate raised her eyebrows. "That could be a problem."

"Though not much of one," I admitted.

"What do you mean?" Cate questioned.

"His story was so full of contradictions and holes, it wouldn't be hard to place doubt in anyone's mind. He's got an alibi, he says he killed Andrew in his office, yet there is no evidence of that. The weapon he said he used isn't likely to have left the injuries he sustained. There are a hundred ways I can argue him out of custody."

Cate's eyes widened. "Wow, we're quite the confident attorney, aren't we?" she quipped.

"Well, Lady Cate, it's crazy, but it just might work," I said with a laugh.

"Gosh, I hope so," Cate said. "We have to act fast, though. We don't have much time."

"You're right. We need to get things in place before I'm due at the police station. They will file charges against Randolph this afternoon unless we can convince them not to. The only way we can do that is to convince Randolph to recant his story. And the only way he'll do that is if he knows Sonia is safe."

"Will retracting his confession be enough for the police to dismiss him as a suspect?"

"Perhaps not outright, but it should shed enough confusion that they will consider other suspects. At least I hope so."

"Well, it's our only option, so let's change and do this!"

"Okay. And if you've got any good luck charms, now's the time to carry them, Lady Cate. Meet you in the usual spot!"

"See you in a few!

I changed and paced the floor as I awaited Cate's arrival.

"Second thoughts?" she asked as she entered the bedroom.

"Nope, not one. Just anxious to get moving."

"Me, too," Cate agreed. "Let's go."

* * *

"Cate!" Sonia exclaimed. "I spent much of my night wondering if I had dreamt you and wondering if you would return."

"We are real," Cate assured her, "and we have a plan."

Sonia listened intently as Cate outlined our plan, summarizing the highlights and positive outcomes. "Do you think this will work?"

"Yes, it will work," Cate pledged, "it has to."

"I trust her," I chimed in. "We'll make it work."

Sonia nodded. "All right, then let us proceed."

"Good," Cate said. "Come." Cate stood, pulling Sonia to her feet. "We must gather your things and move you."

Between the three of us, we assembled Sonia's limited possessions, placing them in a suitcase. "Follow me," Cate said to Sonia, lugging the suitcase with her.

"Be safe," I said before they left.

Cate nodded. "I'll be back as soon as I can to help."

"Okay. I'll do what I can before you're back."

Cate and Sonia disappeared from the tower room and I started my work. I removed my jacket and rolled up my sleeves. I pulled the covers from the bed and shoved them into the dresser. I pushed the desk and dresser as close to the door as I could before I rolled up the area rug and stood it against the wall.

I pulled the blackout curtains from the windows and discarded them into the wardrobe. As I closed the wardrobe doors, Cate returned.

"Wow," Cate marveled, "great job so far!

"Are you sure you're able to do this in that outfit?"

"I'll try. I picked a less cumbersome dress just for the occasion. Come on, we'll move the desk first."

"Right," I said, positioning myself behind the desk, allowing Cate to take the front and walk facing forward. "Ready?"

"Ready. Straight to the unused bedroom."

"And hope no one is there. Okay, on three." I counted to three, and we lifted the desk and carried it to the unused bedroom near the tower stairs. We repeated the process with the dresser, stowing it in a storage room near the tower. Finally, we shoved the mattress in the same storage room and stacked the bed frame in the corner of the tower room. We shuffled several boxes from the storage room to the tower and dumped them around the space, making it appear like the storage area Randolph claimed it to be.

Cate sunk onto a trunk as she caught her breath. "Okay, part one of the plan finished. Sonia is moved, and the tower room is dismantled. No one would suspect someone has lived here for over a decade."

"Now on to part two. You ready?" I asked, holding out my hand to pull Cate up to standing.

Cate nodded, grabbing my hand. "As I'll ever be!"

We trekked to town and entered the police station. I requested to see Randolph, stating Cate wanted to speak with him first. The desk clerk disappeared for a moment before returning and motioning for Cate to follow him. "Mrs. MacKenzie, if you'll follow me."

I offered a nod of encouragement as Cate followed him down the hall. I paced the floor of the entryway as I offered a silent prayer that Cate pulled this off.

After a few minutes, the clerk said, "Mr. MacKenzie, if you'll follow me, you may meet with your client."

I followed him down the hall. Cate passed me in the opposite direction. She reached out to grab my hand. "Good luck," she mouthed.

"Showtime!" I whispered with a grin.

I entered the small interrogation room. Randolph sat at the table. I pulled up a chair next to him.

"It's one hell of a plan Catherine imparted to me, Jack," Randolph said as I took my seat.

"It's a good one," I agreed. "Are you ready?"

"You're certain Sonia is safe?"

"Catherine saw to it herself. She's at the castle hidden in another room known only to me and Cate. As soon as you're released, we'll retrieve her and introduce her to your household as my niece."

Randolph nodded his head. "What of the tower room?"

"Catherine and I dismantled it this morning. It now appears to be the storage room you claimed it was when Catherine inquired about it on our castle tour. It also appears to be a wonderful spot for a clandestine meeting between Andrew and one of his questionable associates. A place where a murder could occur without the household being aware."

"All right, Jack. What must I do?"

"Recant. Unequivocally. You did not murder him. Tell the truth, the same truth you told the night of the murder. Leave the rest to me, but whatever you do, do not waiver."

"Agreed. Shall we get to it?"

I nodded and called for the officers on the case. Abernathy and MacCrae filed into the room moments later.

"Mr. MacKenzie, I understand your client has something to say?"

"Yes, he does."

All eyes turned to Randolph. "I would like to recant my confession," Randolph said.

Both officers stared at Randolph, their expressions aghast. "I did not kill Mr. Forsythe. I am sorry, gentlemen, I do not know what came over me. Though I am able to think clearly now."

"I'm sorry, Lord MacKenzie, am I to understand you are now saying you are not guilty after you've confessed to the crime?"

"Yes," Randolph answered.

"Why in the world would you confess to a crime you did not commit?"

"I felt pressured. Your disruption of my household caused me to panic. I confessed to avoid the upset to my household."

Abernathy's brows furrowed. "You confessed, so we did not search your home? You did not find confessing to murder an upset to your household."

"He's explained he was under duress and not in his right mind when he confessed," I said.

The officers sat stunned for another moment. "Lord MacKenzie, you confessed to a crime. You insisted on it, in fact. And now you expect us to accept your recanting of said statement."

"Yes, we do," I insisted. "In fact, it would be wise for you to collect Lord MacKenzie's statement anew."

He shook his head after a moment, but Abernathy agreed. He shuffled to a blank sheet of paper to take notes.

"All right, Lord MacKenzie. Could you tell us what happened on the night of 31 October?"

"Certainly. I hosted the first Halloween ball with my wife at the castle. We received many guests. I last spoke with Andrew Forsythe at nine-thirty. We spoke for a short time during which I dismissed him."

"Why?" MacCrae interjected.

"It had come to my attention that his behavior was

dishonorable. I do not wish to employ such people, so I dismissed him."

"And his response was?"

"An angry one. He railed against me, threatened me with spreading scandalous rumors."

"And you killed him," MacCrae said in statement form.

"No," Randolph countered. "I informed him his presence was no longer welcome on the estate, he should pack his things and depart at once."

"In the middle of your ball, you dismissed a servant."

"Yes," Randolph confirmed. "I cared not about the party, but more about ensuring his behavior did not continue under my roof."

"And then?"

"I spoke with Mr. and Mrs. MacKenzie for a few moments. I made a few arrangements for serving with three staff members and then returned to the ball."

"Lord MacKenzie," Abernathy said, "you described to us in detail the murder. How do you explain this sudden turn in your account?"

"He's already explained it," I said. "His second account was riddled with contradictions and you know that. It's why you did not charge him…"

"We were about to charge him, Mr. MacKenzie," Abernathy claimed. "We held off at your request."

"You held off because you weren't sure and you damn well know it." I reached across the table and spread his papers out. "Let's take a moment to dissect these other statements, shall we?"

"Mr. MacKenzie, control yourself. You…"

"NO!" I shouted. "My request is not unreasonable. Let us go over in detail each statement from Lord MacKenzie's false confession, and we shall prove it is a fake."

"I would very much like to hear how you will prove this," MacCrae said.

"Fine," I countered. "Then let's get to it, shall we?"

With a grumble, Abernathy consulted his papers. I began before he could. "Contradiction number one: during his confession, Lord MacKenzie stated he spoke with Andrew as early as nine-fifteen in order to provide himself with as much time as he needed to commit the murder and hide the body. However, my wife's statement, my statement and the statements of several others along with Lord MacKenzie's original statement contradict this. At nine-thirty, Lord MacKenzie shared a dance with my wife, making it impossible to have been speaking with Andrew Forsythe before this."

Abernathy shuffled through his papers as I continued. "Contradiction number two: Lord MacKenzie stated he struck the victim with the butt of a pistol then discarded the pistol into the loch the following day. The pistol is inconsistent with the injuries sustained by the victim. And if you check, I am certain you would find said pistol still safe and sound within Lord MacKenzie's desk drawer because he did not, in fact, use it to strike Mr. Forsythe."

Abernathy glared at me as he glanced up from his notes. "Third contradiction: You stated the body sustained injuries consistent with a fall from a height. Lord MacKenzie stated he dropped the body while dragging it to the garden. The injuries from dropping a body a few feet aren't consistent with the injuries Mr. Forsythe sustained.

"Fourth, Lord MacKenzie's alibi is confirmed by three staff members. All of whom saw him shortly after both Mrs. MacKenzie and I spoke with him. He had no time to move the body before or after our conversation, given the timing. Additionally, a close contact crime of this nature would have left blood spattered on the murderer and within the room the murder was committed. No blood was found within Lord MacKenzie's office. You were in it that night and spotted no signs of a struggle or a violent attack. And Lord MacKenzie's clothing had no blood spatters on it.

"Lastly, Lord MacKenzie's first statement is inconsistent with all other statements given that night and the one he just gave you. This is the accurate and truthful statement. Your case against Lord MacKenzie won't hold up anywhere, certainly not in a courtroom. Check your notes, Officer Abernathy. I would suggest you check them carefully before proceeding. It's your case to ruin by charging my client with a crime he could not have committed."

I crossed my arms and leaned back in my chair, staring at the two officers.

"You'll have to excuse us for a moment, gentlemen," Abernathy said. He collected his papers and stood. Without another word, he stalked from the room with MacCrae following him.

"Bravo, Jack," Randolph said. "Do you suppose it'll work?"

"I certainly hope so," I said with a sigh.

CHAPTER 30

November 5
9:42 p.m.

e waited for two hours before Abernathy and MacCrae returned. "Well, gentlemen? Are you ready to release my client?" I questioned.

"Not just yet," Abernathy said as they both settled into their chairs.

A knot formed in my stomach. "We have a few more questions for your client."

We spent the next several hours covering the same ground over and over. I pointed out the inconsistencies with the confession again. I also reminded them of Andrew's shady connections. As the afternoon waned, their questions ceased. The two officers stepped from the room again, leaving us alone.

"I'm sorry, Jack," Randolph said as they departed. "I may have cost us greatly with my mistaken confession."

"Let's hope for the best," I said.

Within thirty minutes, Abernathy returned alone. He

approached Randolph and unlocked the handcuffs on his wrists. "You are free to go, Lord MacKenzie. BUT… do not leave the area. Our investigation is not yet concluded. Though we have no plans to charge you at this time."

I smiled to myself. We won!

"I understand," Randolph answered them. "I have no plans to leave and I hope you catch the person who did this. I apologize for the delay I've caused. Though, as I said, I was not in my right mind."

"I should charge you with obstruction…" Abernathy began.

"Just a moment," I began.

"I am not, Mr. MacKenzie, calm down. We may need to question some of your staff again."

"Whatever you need," Randolph agreed.

Abernathy nodded to him. "Then you are free to go." He motioned toward the open door.

"Just a moment," I repeated. "Will you be troubling my client any further?"

"Other than speaking with the staff, I doubt it, Mr. MacKenzie. In our review, we found several reports of Mr. Forsythe's unscrupulous ties."

"What about a search of the grounds?" Randolph questioned. "This whole mess started because I did not want our lives turned upside down."

"Not necessary," Abernathy admitted. "I'd doubt the murder weapon remains on your estate, Lord MacKenzie. Most likely the dubious character who committed this crime fled with it and is long gone."

Randolph and I stood and made our way out of the police station. Randolph glanced at the setting sun as he filled his lungs with the fresh air.

"I never imagined I'd see it again," he admitted. "Thank you, Jack. Both you and Catherine."

"You're welcome, Randolph," I said. "Now, let's get back to the castle. We still have the second half of the plan to carry out."

"Yes, Sonia," Randolph answered. "I am anxious to get her settled."

We walked to the castle with Randolph setting a hard pace. Randolph pushed through the front doors and into the foyer the moment we arrived. Victoria raced into the entry-way, with Cate following her.

"Randolph!" she exclaimed, rushing to him. "Oh, my darling husband." She threw her arms around his neck in a full embrace. "How are you? Have they mistreated you?"

"Victoria, I'm fine, just fine."

Cate glanced at me, a smile on her face. I understood her emotion. The heartwarming scene made the hours of hard work worth it.

Victoria released Randolph, turning to embrace me. "How can I ever thank you, cousin Jack? You have my eternal gratitude."

"We're not out of the woods yet, to coin a phrase from my wife, but most of the difficulty has passed. The investigation's focus should move from Randolph. They shouldn't trouble you anymore."

"Oh, what a spectacle I am," Victoria said, standing back, wiping tears from her cheeks.

"Shall we go into the sitting room?" Randolph suggested, "I could use a drink."

"As could I," I agreed.

Randolph poured drinks for everyone after we entered the sitting room. Thomson arrived to satisfy any requests.

"Champagne," Randolph ordered, "four glasses. We are celebrating tonight!" Thomson left to retrieve the request. Once delivered, poured and each of us held a glass, Randolph toasted, "To Jack. Catherine, your husband is a legal genius."

They all raised their glasses to me. "Well, I don't know about that, sir," I said, after sipping my champagne. "But you certainly tested my mettle."

"No need to be modest, my boy. You got me out of quite a tight spot. I made a serious miscalculation, and you handled it with ease."

"We can never repay you, either of you, cousins," Victoria said. "Catherine, you are to be commended, too. Were it not for you, I wouldn't have survived. And Jack, dear Jack, I cannot thank you enough."

"It is our pleasure," I answered. Then joked, "Besides, I had to help Randolph. I need a favor from him."

"We'll do anything, just name it," Victoria said.

"Thank you for being so accommodating without yet knowing the request," I said.

"I know the request and I hardly think we're being overly accommodating," Randolph said.

"You know it?" Victoria asked, cocking her head.

"I do." Randolph nodded. "We had plenty of time to discuss it while the police sorted through things."

"Are you both going to play coy? What is it?"

"I've just learned my niece, Sonia, my sister's child, has been orphaned. My sister died birthing Sonia, and now my brother-in-law has passed away in an accident," I explained.

"Oh, how terrible for the poor child," Victoria lamented.

"Yes, it is most unfortunate. As her next-of-kin, the duty falls to me to look after her. With my need to travel, it may become difficult. While I realize the imposition this places on you, I beseeched Randolph if she may spend some time at the castle until such time that Catherine and I are settled and can take her in. Perhaps, she could provide companionship for you, Victoria."

"Imposition? Nonsense!" Victoria exclaimed. "She is

family. There's no imposition at all. We would welcome her. How delightful to meet a new family member."

"I concur," Randolph agreed. "It's poppycock to think it an imposition!"

"What is her age?" Victoria inquired.

"She is nearly sixteen," I responded.

"Oh, what fun we shall have!" Victoria exclaimed. "You were right to come to us. She should not be unsettled, traveling about the country at this age. She must be guided, taught, supported and trained. We shall make sure she is raised to make a fine match and become a true lady. Do not give it a second thought, cousins. I will see to it all. When will she arrive?"

"In fact, she is already here. I traveled to retrieve her last evening, returning early this morning with Sonia."

"Oh, you must send for her at once! And I must send for my dressmaker. We must buy her a new dress or two, perhaps even three, for the upcoming holiday season. We will travel to London, we will attend many holiday parties before and after the new year."

"As you can see, cousin Jack," Randolph said, "my wife has the situation well in hand."

"Yes." I chuckled. "It appears so. In all seriousness though, I am fortunate to count you as family."

"Well, I agree with my wife. Sonia should be sent for at once. I shall tell Thomson to set an extra place for dinner. Please, cousin, might you retrieve her tonight?"

"I should be glad to."

"Oh, Randolph, please have Mrs. Carmichael prepare the bedroom down the hall from mine for Sonia. You don't mind if she stays with us beginning tonight, do you, cousin Jack?

"Not at all. It would be preferable that she become settled prior to our departure. This would give her a few weeks to become comfortable while we are here to visit. I shall retrieve her now."

I left the room and made a show of slamming the front door behind me. I waited several moments before I sneaked back into the foyer. I darted up the main staircase and navigated to the bedroom Cate hid Sonia in.

Almost out of the woods, I reflected, as I pushed through the bedroom door. The room appeared undisturbed. For a moment, I wondered if I entered the wrong room. I hurried across the room to the closet. After a quiet knock, I peeked inside. I spotted nothing.

Had I gotten the room wrong? "Sonia?" I called just above a whisper.

"Jack?" she answered. She revealed herself, hidden in a back corner behind a trunk.

"Yes," I said with a smile. "Come. I'm here to take you to Randolph. We've explained everything. We'll introduce you as my niece and you'll live here."

"They've agreed?" she questioned.

"Yes. Randolph is most anxious to have you settled."

A small smile crossed her lips, and she approached. "Quiet now, we must sneak from the castle and around to the front." I grabbed her suitcase and carried it for her.

She nodded and together we crept through the halls, then outside. We circled around to the front drive. We wandered up the gravel driveway and entered. I set the suitcase in the foyer.

"Ready?" I asked.

Sonia nodded. I pushed through the doors into the sitting room. "May I present my niece, Sonia Morgan?"

"Sonia, my dear child, come in. Please, call me Uncle Randolph," Randolph said.

"I should like that, Uncle Randolph," Sonia said, her voice barely above a whisper.

I guided her forward as Victoria rose. "Sonia, welcome!" She approached the girl and embraced her, adding a kiss on her cheek. "I am your Aunt Victoria. We are so pleased to welcome you into our family and our home. Please, come and sit down." Victoria led her to the loveseat to sit. "Your journey was no doubt taxing on you. Are you exhausted from it?"

"I am rather tired," Sonia admitted.

"Poor child. We shall go to dinner soon, you can retire afterward to rest. I've had a bedroom prepared for you near mine. I look so forward to your stay. We shall have such fun together, Sonia!" Victoria held Sonia's hands in hers, offering a wide, bright smile.

"Thank you for your graciousness, Aunt Victoria," Sonia answered.

"There is no need for gratitude, Sonia. We are family. Oh, I hope you enjoy fashion. I cannot wait to have my dressmaker in for an appointment with you. You are a very pretty girl," Victoria said, fussing with her hair. "Your complexion is quite light but very attractive. You shall do well in bold colors."

"I shall be excited to have a new dress of any color.

Victoria beamed. "Oh, no, my dear, not *A* new dress. We shall buy many new dresses for you. You shall need them, we shall attend many events."

Sonia smiled for the first time. I must admit that little smile almost brought tears to my eyes. Though I didn't cry, I assure you. But the scene was touching. I was pleased to have been a part of its creation.

We enjoyed dinner and afterward, Victoria and Cate disappeared to settle Sonia. Randolph poured another drink for me. "I do not know how to thank you, Jack," Randolph said. "This is more than I could have ever hoped for."

"It is my pleasure," I assured him. "In some ways, I suppose your confession prompted this resolution."

"So, you are admitting my confession was, in fact, a good idea?" Randolph quipped.

"I would not go that far, sir," I answered with a chuckle. "But I am pleased it has worked out so well."

Cate and Victoria joined us shortly after.

"Have her all settled, my dear?" Randolph asked.

"Settled and snug in her new bed," Victoria answered. "And do not worry, cousin Jack, as I told Catherine, I shall have Sonia prepared to make a fine match in short order. She shall have the upbringing of a fine lady. Oh, Jack, has she any musical training? It is sometimes a good skill for young ladies to possess, it makes them seem clever."

"I do not believe she has, Victoria," I answered.

"Randolph, we should arrange for her to learn pianoforte. I do hope she might show some skill for it. We shall see!"

"Of course, my dear. Whatever you suggest."

"I shall make a list."

"Wonderful, my dear," Randolph said. "Well, cousin," Randolph addressed me, "as you can see, we have the situation well in hand. I hope this sets your mind at ease."

"It does, sir, it does. I shall feel most comfortable leaving her in your care. You have taken a great weight from my mind."

"We both appreciate it very much," Cate chimed in. "We shall take our leave for the evening. It has been a trying day, I'm sure you both would like to relax."

"Indeed," Victoria answered, "as has it been for both of you. Please get some rest. Will you visit tomorrow?"

"Yes," I said. "I'd like to see how Sonia has settled. Perhaps we shall stop in the afternoon for tea."

"We shall look forward to seeing you then," Randolph agreed. "I shall walk you to the door."

We left Victoria in the sitting room while Randolph led us to the foyer. "Jack, Catherine, I cannot thank you enough. I shall forever be in your debt."

"Save your thanks for when we are sure you are cleared of all charges, Randolph," I said.

"All in due time, my boy, all in due time. Now, I shall see you tomorrow. You should have an unfettered path to your destination if you go now."

"See you tomorrow, Randolph," Cate said.

We ascended the stairs, winding through the halls to the bedroom closet. We used the timepiece to return to our time. I breathed my customary sigh of relief.

"WOW!" Cate exclaimed. "I want to hear all about it."

"I want to take a nap." I sighed. "Whew, I can't believe it's only been an hour."

"Oh, come on," Cate teased, "I've been waiting all day."

"Actually, you've only been waiting an hour," I corrected.

"How are you not excited?"

I chuckled. "Okay, okay. I'll admit it, it felt rather good helping both Randolph and Sonia today."

"Rather good? That's it?" Cate asked, raising her eyebrows.

"It felt pretty damned good," I admitted with a laugh.

"So, out with it!"

"At least let me change!" I complained.

"Okay, okay, meet in the library as usual?"

"Meet in the library, as usual, Lady Cate."

When I arrived in the library, Cate awaited me.

"Wow, Lady Cate, you beat me. You must be anxious to hear this story!"

"I am! I don't understand how you did it, Jack. Now, come on, tell me every detail! Don't leave anything out."

"Okay, okay," I agreed, sinking into an armchair. Cate perched on the edge of her seat with bated breath. "It wasn't too difficult. Once Randolph stopped insisting he was guilty, I succeeded in convincing the police they needed to consider other suspects."

"Did Randolph need much persuasion on your part?"

"Only an assurance that Sonia was safe. I told him you had seen to it yourself, that you'd never let anything happen to the girl."

"And then what? He just told the police to cancel his confession?"

"No, it was more difficult than that. He recanted his statement. The police were not happy. They reviewed his statement over and over from when he confessed and his subsequent questioning. We pointed out all the inconsistencies, which they themselves questioned on both occasions. Then I asked them to review the original statements taken from the night of the party. Randolph's new statement matched that one and the other witness testimony. They realized, as we did when we went through the same exercise, that it was impossible for Randolph to have killed Andrew."

"So, he's off the hook, right?"

"Well, they asked him not to leave the area just yet and they haven't officially removed him from the suspect list, but I expect it's only a matter of time. Still, we should check back until he is no longer considered a suspect. Or until the investigation is closed, assuming that's before the end of the year."

"Wait, did I just hear you suggest we SHOULD time travel?"

I laughed. "Yes, my dear Lady Cate, I suggested it. I want to see this through. It's my first big legal win."

"Yes, apparently you are quite the legal genius."

"You know it."

"Did the police mention any other suspects?"

"Yes, they did. I inquired after telling them I hoped my client would no longer be bothered by this. They said they may poke around the grounds but doubted they would find much."

"Because it's been too long since the murder?"

"No, they didn't presume the murder weapon was on the estate."

"Really?" Cate raised her eyebrows in surprise.

"Yes. From the eyewitness accounts of that night, several people told the police they had seen Andrew meeting with another man earlier that evening. The man wasn't someone anyone was acquainted with, but they had seen him with Andrew once or twice before. They appeared to be arguing. The police assume the man was an associate of Andrew's and murdered him over whatever they were arguing about."

"Sonia mentioned seeing Andrew meeting with someone, too."

"Right. Probably the same man. Based on his description, the police suspect he was a rather disreputable fellow. They assume Andrew was involved in some nefarious things and it cost him his life."

"Wonder what will happen when they find him and he says he's innocent. He may even have an alibi."

"I doubt they'll ever find him. With the trouble, he's probably long gone never to return to avoid any suspicion."

"Gosh, I hope so," Cate said.

"Relax, Cate, we stand a good chance. And a far better chance than we did when Randolph was professing his guilt."

Cate contemplated for a moment. "Hmm, wow, I still can't believe this worked."

"Hey!" I exclaimed, "what do you mean you can't believe it worked? You insisted this plan would work!"

"Well," Cate said with a shrug, "I hoped it would work,

but now that it did, I'm shocked it went so smoothly. I mean, Randolph confessed, he was insistent. Then he just recanted, and they accepted it."

"They had no choice. His confession was questionable from the start. That's why I had such an easy time getting them to agree not to charge him right away. Even they questioned if it would stick."

"Wow," Cate whispered, stunned into silence after considering the breadth of the situation.

"Now it's just a waiting game to get the all-clear, which I hope comes soon."

"Me, too. You know, we're approaching the end of the year, it's sad to realize we won't be able to visit anymore."

I nodded. "Yes, I can't believe I'm about to admit to this but I will miss them."

"Me, too," Cate said, sighing. "Oh, well, I suppose we should start our day… again."

"I suppose so. I'll tell you one thing I won't miss is living two days in the time of only one."

"You and me both. It's evening to me but we haven't even had lunch yet. At least it's helping my terrible sleep habits. I sleep the entire night!"

"And it only took time travel to cure your insomnia. Who would have ever guessed traveling through time would benefit one's health?"

Cate gave me an amused look. "Back to research for me and preparing for Molly's arrival."

"Have you heard from her? I'll bet she is excited."

"I have. She's already sent some of her things."

"I'll bet she would have stayed here and never gone back if she could have."

"I agree. She's counting the days down."

"Well," I said, standing, "let me know when her things

arrive, I'll get them moved. If you need anything else done before she's due here, let me know, I'll get right on it."

"Thanks, Jack."

So, there you have it! My first legal battle in the books AND in the win column. We'll return tomorrow to check on the situation but it seems to be well in hand. And I, for one, am grateful. This double life is exhausting! I barely got this typed without falling asleep. But it's in the record and now I can rest.

CHAPTER 31

November 7
7:48 p.m.

I met Cate mid-afternoon to return to 1856. We met Victoria and Randolph for tea in the solarium. When we arrived, we found Victoria and Sonia discussing Sonia's musical education. As we entered, Sonia stood and curtsied.

"Good day, Uncle Jack and Aunt Catherine," she said.

Victoria smiled and nodded as she took her seat again. She beamed at me and Cate, giving us a wink. "Come in and sit down, cousins. Sonia and I were just discussing furthering her education. She is keen on learning an instrument."

We sat at the table. "Hello, Sonia. You look well," Cate said.

"Indeed," I added, "how was your first night in the castle?"

"Splendid," Sonia answered. Her eyes sparkled with renewed interest in life. "I slept well. The bed is incredibly comfortable."

"I had Bryson alter this dress for her," Victoria said. "To tide her over until my dressmaker can create some new things for her. The color does well on her. It always made me sallow. Would you agree, Catherine?"

"Quite fitting," Cate concurred.

"I've already sent for the dressmaker and to acquire a piano-forte instructor. Sonia may be keen on learning a language, too. She is quite clever," Victoria said.

"I'm so pleased," I said as Randolph entered the room.

"Well, cousins, I'm so pleased you could join us," he said as he approached the table.

I stood, shaking his hand. "Randolph," I said, "Sonia looks well. I am so pleased with Victoria's plans for her."

"As am I!" Randolph admitted as we both seated ourselves. "I am afraid, however, I have some bad news."

"Oh no, what is it?" Cate asked. My heart raced at the admission.

"I shall no longer require your legal counsel, Jack. The police have cleared me of the murder and removed me from the suspect list. I know how you shall miss sparring with them."

"That's fantastic news, Randolph," I said, clapping him on the back. "Although, I will miss the scrapping."

"I could do without it," Victoria noted.

"What of the case?" I asked.

"They are searching for some dubious character by the name of Simon Dupree. Involved in all sorts of scandal, that one. He was seen on the property multiple times, including the fateful night. I doubt the police will ever catch up with him. Long gone at the first hint of trouble, I'm sure."

"Undoubtedly," I agreed.

"Please, may we speak of something lighter?" Victoria pleaded.

"Agree," Cate chimed in.

We spent the meal making light conversation. I planned to announce we would leave the area in the next week or two, though a pang of guilt plagued me. I truly felt sorry for Cate as I watched her interacting with the only family she had left. Still, it must be done, so at the conclusion of the meal, I made the announcement.

At the conclusion of our evening, Randolph offered to walk us to the door, mentioning he would like a moment alone with us before we departed. We strode to his office, and he closed the door behind us.

"With the year drawing to a close," Randolph began, "I suppose we shan't be meeting much more."

"Sadly, no," Cate said. "As the new year arrives, the time clock will reset, as I understand it. Therefore, our travels using this specific rip would bring us back to relive this same year."

"Correct," Randolph agreed.

Cate was silent for a moment, composing herself. "I… that is, we…" she stumbled. "I wish there was another way. It would be nice to visit."

"I cannot offer any solutions. But perhaps…" he began.

"Yes?" Cate asked in earnest.

"You may find it helpful to consult with Douglas. To this day, I do not understand how he tamed the power in this castle."

"Douglas MacKenzie, the original castle owner?" I asked.

"Yes, old Doug, my grandfather. A crafty bugger, that one. If anyone can offer you a way, he can."

"I promise to look into that!" Cate vowed.

"Please, sir, don't encourage her," I joked.

"Ah, laddie, apologies, but my encouragement, or lack of, will not change her mind."

"Probably not," I answered.

"Definitely not. She's a MacKenzie, we're a strong-willed lot!"

"You've got that right," I agreed.

"I for one am glad of it. Without her willfulness, I might be in prison."

"Aye, that's a likely bet, sir."

"On that note, I wanted to say thank you. Thank you to both of you. I cannot ever repay you for what you've done."

"There's no repayment necessary, Randolph," Cate said to him. "We are so pleased to have helped." Cate offered him a wide smile.

"Even so, my family and I are indebted to you. And now, before this moment turns maudlin, particularly for Catherine, let us part ways. I hope to see you at least one more time before the year is out."

"You will," Cate promised.

"So, it's goodbye, for now, Catherine and Jack. Until we meet again," Randolph said.

We said our goodbyes, promising to see each other at least once more before we returned to the closet and our own time.

CHAPTER 32

November 15
7:17 p.m.

We made time for one last trip to 1856 today. Cate and I enjoyed a visit with Randolph, Victoria and Sonia. Without any additional legal trouble, the MacKenzies of this era thrived. Under Victoria's guidance, Sonia blossomed. Both she and Randolph would live full lives.

As resistant as I was, I'm proud to have been a part of this. Cate and I made a difference in the world. A measurable one. We preserved and saved a man's life along with changing a young woman's. I'm loathe to admit this to Cate, but I enjoyed myself.

Why not tell her, you wonder? Because as pleased as I am, I'm still not a fan of time traveling. Gosh, I hope Lady Cate doesn't find any other mysteries lurking on this estate to solve. But rest assured, if she does, I'll record it in this journal.

The End